hard ticket

New Writing Made in Newfoundland

EDITED BY **LISA MOORE**

BREAKWATER
P.O. Box 2188, St. John's, NL, Canada, A1C 6E6
www.breakwaterbooks.com

COPYRIGHT © 2022 Lisa Moore
ISBN 978-1-55081-827-7

LIBRARY AND ARCHIVES CANADA CATALOGUING IN PUBLICATION
Title: Hard ticket : new writing made in Newfoundland / edited by Lisa Moore.
Names: Moore, Lisa, 1964- editor.
Description: Short stories.
Identifiers: Canadiana 20220248974 | ISBN 9781550818277 (softcover)
Subjects: LCSH: Short stories, Canadian—Newfoundland and Labrador. | LCSH: Canadian fiction—21st century. | CSH: Short stories, Canadian (English)—Newfoundland and Labrador. | CSH: Canadian fiction (English)—21st century.
Classification: LCC PS8329.5.N3 H37 2022 | DDC C813/.01089718—dc23

All rights reserved. No part of this publication may be reproduced, stored in a retrieval system or transmitted, in any form or by any means, without the prior written consent of the publisher or a licence from the Canadian Copyright Licensing Agency (Access Copyright). For an Access Copyright licence, visit www.accesscopyright.ca or call toll free 1-800-893-5777.

We acknowledge the support of the Canada Council for the Arts.
We acknowledge the financial support of the Government of Canada through the Department of Heritage and the Government of Newfoundland and Labrador through the Department of Tourism, Culture, Arts and Recreation for our publishing activities.

Printed and bound in Canada.

Breakwater Books is committed to choosing papers and materials for our books that help to protect our environment. To this end, this book is printed on recycled paper that is certified by the Forest Stewardship Council®.

hard ticket *noun* (Nfld)
a lively character, a tough or headstrong person, someone not easily controlled.

contents

Lisa Moore   Introduction... **7**

Michelle Porter   Snowblower... **13**

Carrie-Jane Williams   Past Tenses... **21**

Allison Graves   Sugar... **27**

Elizabeth Hicks   Ten Frames Forever... **33**

Tzu-Hao Hsu   Twilight Airs, Iron, Water... **45**

Benjamin C. Dugdale   Starecase... **53**

Xaiver Michael Campbell   Eight Months to a Year... **71**

Heidi Wicks   The Flat Freshie Blue-Star Test... **85**

Olivia Robinson   Effie... **99**

William Ping   Lord Gushue's Reign of Terror... **109**

Sobia Shaheen Shaikh   You-Cee... **117**

Matthew Hollett   The City Wears Thin... **137**

Prajwala Dixit   एकत्र Ēkatra... **151**

Bridget Canning   The Years the Locusts Have Eaten... **175**

Terry Doyle   What Kind of Dog Is He?... **187**

Carmella Gray-Cosgrove   Remains of Conception... **195**

Jim McEwen   Lost Villages... **207**

introduction

LISA MOORE

Blobs of snow bend the branches and the white ground is splotched with violet shadows and islands of brilliant light. At the end the tunnel formed by the branches overhead is an obliterating oval of fierce sunlight. A splat of snow falls off a branch onto my shoulder, like somebody patting me. A bunch of chickadees chirp all at once and fly up, a blur of feather and consequence.

A story is, in part, a spontaneous combustion, a consummation, the result of the atmosphere it's born into—it is order out of chaos and it holds forth until another story overtakes it. One of the little birds has come to the very tip of the branch, quite close to my face, and turns its head and blinks at me. Through a telepathy, loud as a boom box, the bird tells me that a story is an antidote. But that's just its opinion.

The stories in this anthology come into the hands of readers at a particular moment in history, and these confluences of bright and the darkest of dark dictate, in no small part, how the reader will receive the story.

I have three English setters with me, and one is still, head hanging low, front paw lifted, and off, a liquid flash of sleek silver coat, into the thrashing underbrush. A rabbit, a rabbit darts across the path, paws barely touching down—a story is style, the rabbit says, it is speed and grace and suspension and fear and resolution. It is the play between time holding still and the kind of time that is delivered to us with the James Webb telescope, stars a billion years in the past (or is it the future)? A telescope with a gazillion mirrors at odd angles so reality is concentrated. Apparently, Canadian scientists were in charge of focusing the thing. It is slathered with gold, go figure.

I keep walking toward that oval of light, my pupils dilating and contracting.

Yesterday I watched every news video I could find of the convoy of truckers crossing the country. They are anti-vaccine and anti-mask, anti-mandate, anti-your-mother-wears-army-boots and anti-gluten and anti-carbon tax. A convoy that began in Canada is spreading across the globe. They are full of anger. They have been menacing, racist. They have children among them, who they nudge to the foreground while they hold the line and chant *freedom*, a story warped and imported. They have porta-potties and saunas and hot tubs. The image of idling tractors, nose to tail, tires so large and brutal they might nudge down a brick wall, a store front, a person. They have noise machines on their trucks loud enough to cause a vibration that rises through the sidewalk, through the soles of winter boots, designed to frighten moose off the highway from miles away. They blast these horns all day and night.

All the things Canadians believed we were armed against, a flimsy story we told ourselves about being polite, anti-racist, fair-minded, and law-abiding.

But the tractors and trucks, huffing exhaust in the cold air, seem to lie in wait.

Full of might, what we might become. And sure enough, the muscle-bulged arm of the law eventually comes down, creating a new law, a new story, that might be pretty dangerous if unleashed by the wrong regime, at the wrong time, to the wrong audience. And it took its time, the law lollygagged, in direct contrast with the way the law has often dealt with Indigenous protest—fast, violent.

There's a new unleashing around the world—what Freud might call the return of the repressed, the things we wish to tamp down but that pop back up, no matter how hard we push against them.

Russians on the border of Ukraine, the news says: attack imminent. Countries rally. A bare-chested bully riding a horse is demanding his right to a story.

I am stomping through this tunnel of newly fallen snow, branches overhead, asking myself what elements I was looking for when asking for the stories collected here. What I learned from them about shape, about content, about the adjective and active or passive verbs, about power and the powerless and everyone in between.

I wanted to hear the voice of the author. A story is always an effort to capture the human voice, its timbre and cadence, its breath. I wanted stories the reader experienced through her nose and eyes and ears and fingertips, and of course, all the organs. These writers are aware of the cudgel a semi-colon can be. The drunken extravagance of an exclamation mark. How a run-on sentence can make the reader's heart hurry to catch up. I wanted stories that forced a blush in the reader cheeks, caused fear and recognition. Gripped. Held fast. And this kind of story, I suspected, was a question of style. What is style?

When I was thirteen, I was on a galloping horse, a horse that had been pent up in a barn after a snowstorm, a wild horse at the best of times, a horse desperate to get out. Snow drifts everywhere; glitter on the trees, all sparkle, sunbursts, purity. The horse took off. It was easy at first, when the animal had to reckon with tall drifts, busting through with her chest and high, prancing forelegs, haunches bunching and springing in slow motion, but when we hit the ploughed, glassy highway, the trot broke out, we were in the centre of the road, I was slammed up and down, hanging on, afraid of whatever traffic was coming beyond the blind turn. Then trot gave way to canter and canter, to gallop, a run-on sentence, and the horse left the yellow line to fly under some low-hanging branches and one of those branches caught me by the throat and I was on my back on the ground with the wind knocked out of me.

I could not breathe, exclamation mark. The blue sky and white clouds were bluer and whiter than ever before. I struggled to breathe; but there was no oxygen for the longest time, a few seconds?

But there had been a moment before, when the bumpiness of a trot changed from a canter to a gallop, and though I believed we would slam into a transport truck and I would be flattened like a paper doll, the gallop was like silk or milk or something flowing, charged, pure, and the horse and I were a united thing. Form and content bound, breathing together, the materiality of language as much a part of the story as what was actually happening. Voice and content in equal measure—that is a story.

A story is the opposite of this: the harassment of the staff and residents of the Ottawa Shepherds of Good Hope homeless shelter, casting racial slurs, blocking emergency entrances, as members of the convoy in Ottawa did. Because a story is full of nuance. A story listens while it speaks. A story is multifaceted, slips inside the cells of the reader's imagination, attaches with an always adapting spike. A story is horse and rider. Reader and writer. A story is the deployment of a dash, a gallop and the obdurate inarguable stop of a period, the cold pavement, harder than hard; it is the gasp after we hold our breath or have it knocked out of us. And we have all come to understand the intricate machinery and miracle of drawing breath.

Every story grows from the seed of the stories that came before. It's impossible to paint a tree without referencing all the paintings of trees that preceded the present tree, and all the different kinds of trees ever. Every artwork is a variant. A retelling. Every young girl who falls off a horse stands in a long line of girls falling off horses, and yet every horse and girl, every fall, is unique.

There's another news clip, a feel-good story, thank heavens, of a young moose that has fallen through a high bank of snow into a river rushing below and it can't get out. Four men are determined to rescue it. Ropes are looped around the ungainly bundle of bone, shoulder and knee, oversized head, every bit of the flank aquiver but also still, almost dead from fear, in a coffin of snow and tumbling water, the horror obvious in the bright rolling eye of an animal in shock. But the men pull, and the young moose is freed, ajangle with grace, a knock-kneed discombobulated trot over the snowbank and out of the frame of somebody's phone camera. That's a story.

I watch this moose clip again and again—and can't help but think of the folk song "Tickle Cove Pond"—a horse named Kitty has fallen through the ice and the men of the community try to haul her out. Lay hold William Oldford, lay hold William White, lay hold of the cordage and pull all your might.

We understand the young moose through old Kitty in the folk song, who also takes a dip and is pulled out just in time.

And I rise up from the cold hard pavement and watch the haunches of my own wild horse gallop down the highway of my childhood until it is just a dot in the distance.

The story, a shadow of the one that came before, is altered, made new.

And these stories, which come at the end of a pandemic, what we hope is a kind of end—there is, at least, a fierce light at the end of the tunnel—the easing up, when we all had the breath knocked out of us at the same time, a terrible unified gasp, when our worst nightmares came to the surface, when we were undone and held on and pulled with all our might, these stories are also new. Also fierce. Full of light. Voice. Style.

And you, the reader, what you bring makes them new again and again.

snowblower

MICHELLE PORTER

I'd wanted to kill my father before my mother served dessert. But the Richards dropped by. I sat at the table with Jesse and Leo and Mom, waiting for my dad to get through the usual jokes. Dad liked to think he was funny.

"How long you home for this time?" Of course Leo had to ask. My dad guffawed. That's the only word for it. His laugh sounded like it could be a hippo's mating cry. He guffawed so suddenly my mom, who was sitting beside me, squeaked in surprise, or it could have been fear.

The guffaw turned into a coughing fit. We waited for him to finish, not speaking and not looking at each other. He wasn't in a hurry. He kept on coughing for a long time just for fun, because he liked to show he could keep everybody waiting.

Then he yelled, "How long? Until I'm in my grave." I don't know if they really thought that was funny, but they all laughed. An audience always encourages him. He banged the table with his fist and shouted to Leo, who was sitting opposite him at our narrow table, "this time, there's no getting away." I waited until they were done laughing and saying to each other how Melissa had come home for a couple of months and stayed in the basement for two years and Rob from up the road was probably still sleeping all day in that back room, though his mom had died and the house had been sold over the summer.

"Just a couple of weeks," I said.

Mom got up and brought the cake to the table. She'd already taken it out of the plastic packaging and put it onto a proper serving plate, blue with a fading gold rim. The cake was covered in these red sugar flowers. She plunged a knife into the cake and really hacked it to pieces.

"It's chocolate," she said. She tipped a piece onto a paper plate and pushed it toward me. This was her way of apologizing for Dad. I didn't want it, the cake or the apology.

"Who else?" she asked.

They all said "me." She licked pink icing from her fingers and filled their plates.

I focused on glowering in the general direction of the Richards.

"Oh, the sourpuss face on that one. Look at it," my father crooned, as though I was a baby.

"Dad!" I puffed—and I would have said a lot more, way too much actually, but my mom interrupted.

"Why so pouty tonight, sweetie? You're not sleeping, are you? We'll get you to bed early tonight." She pulled at the ends of her hair nervously, her eyes shifting from me to Dad. I wasn't going to let that stop me. Even though I'd planned on getting Dad outside, I was going to let him have it right there. I took a steadying breath, preparing.

Then the front door opened.

"That Matt?" my father shouted. My mother rushed out of the kitchen and down the hallway to the front door. Matt's seven years younger than me. "He's on exams," my father told Leo and Jesse.

"Exams?" Leo asked.

"Exams," confirmed my dad.

"What kind of exams?"

"Exams, exams. Who cares what kind?" That kind of killed the conversation and we just sat and listened to the sounds of the boots, the coat, and the front closet for a minute.

Mom came back in and told the table: "he says the exams went well. That's just the word he used. He said 'well.'" Matt came in after her in soggy, mismatching socks, one of them mine. He could do exams but he couldn't get his socks to match or keep them dry in winter.

Mom looked up at Matt, "Isn't that right, sweetie? Well. You said you did well."

Matt shrugged, all humble. "I don't know. I think so, Mom. I won't know until they mark them and put the results up."

Mom said something about cake and sit down and she went to get an extra chair and set him up between me and her, then set herself down to admire how well he ate cake. Dad asked for the Christmas music but Mom was too busy watching Matt eat the pink-and-brown supermarket cake so I got up and put on my dad's favourite album, *A Country Christmas*. It was a nice break from his other favourite, *A Holiday round the Bay* or something like that. A man who sounded like he was wearing a cowboy hat and jeans that squished his junk started crooning "White Christmas." I sat back down.

"Sure, it's gonna be a white Christmas this year," Jesse said. She was wiping her plate with her fingers to get at the last of the crumbs and icing, then licking her fingers clean again. She had to be careful with her manicured nails, done up red and sparkly.

"Lotta snow," Leo agreed. "They say there'll be a pile tonight." My dad looked at my uneaten piece of cake.

"You gonna eat that?" I shook my head. He said something about me being too skinny, which isn't true, by the way, and he took my piece of cake for himself.

"Leo, your heart condition," my mom chimed in, on cue.

"Oh, cake won't hurt his heart," Matt said.

"Listen to the boy," my dad said. "He's doing exams." Then they asked him to tell them about his exams. Matt made a long story out of that. You wouldn't believe how funny exams could be. Then, what was that old friend of his, Tom Wazzit, up to? And someone had let them know he had a new girlfriend?

"You got yourself a new girlfriend? Come on. You wouldn't share with your old dad, would you? I need something young and soft again." Leo had a good laugh. Mom frowned at first but she forced a smile.

"Oh, it's true, you know. All the young women would line up for your dad," she said to Matt, forgetting I was there. Matt told us all he didn't fancy sharing this one with Dad, but there was another one he might slip into Dad's bed one night. When the laughter petered out, Mom said, anyway, when was he going to bring her around to meet his parents? Was Matt ashamed of where he came from? Etc., etc.

The sound of snow falling kept me awake all night.

It was maddening. Like a radio tuned between stations. The dead-air static and the murmuring voices you think you could understand if you listened closely enough or if you turned the knob just a bit.

I went to bed in my clothes and I swear I'd just drifted off when I heard my dad. He was in the kitchen, opening drawers or cupboards, getting his first coffee of the day. He's always the first up. I waited until he was out the door before I got out of bed.

I saw through the window that it was still snowing heavily. But my dad always said that living here, you got to clear it as it's snowing, before it gets too bad, or before it turned to rain. He'd be stationed at the window all day during a blizzard and be out clearing up the snow as soon as it got above a centimetre on the driveway and sidewalks. He'd get so fussed up about it he'd even do the neighbours' walkway because they always slept in and sometimes didn't shovel for days in a row. "It'll freeze up," he'd shout at their house through the kitchen window, "and then what? That rain'll turn it all to ice. How will you shovel it then?" I might be leaving out a few of the profanities he liked to use.

Anyway, Mom and him got themselves a riding snowblower for Christmas this year. I don't know where they got the money from. Mom would never use it, we all knew that, but she was worried about his heart condition so she was happy with it. He hadn't had a chance to get it out of the shed yet. Dad turned it on as I stepped out the back door. The security light on the shed lit up most of the backyard, but not the corner by the back door where I was. I loitered in the shadows, watching my dad as he fussed over the blower, patting it here and stroking it there to make sure that it was working all right. The falling snow was light and airy and achingly beautiful. I felt for a moment the way I did as a kid in church, in the pews listening to the visiting Christmas choir sing about the glories and the miracles and the love of Christ. Oh, God.

Then the wind blew in, whipping the snow into a frenzy, and I was glad that I'd put on the full gear: snow pants, jacket, toque, and everything. I grabbed the steel snow shovel, the old heavy one Dad had left behind.

Dad was starting with the path that led from the shed to the back of the house. When I stepped into the light, he yelled something at me. I ignored it. The sound of the snowblower was deafening. The snow whipped around in the wind. The drifts by the fence were almost as high as my waist, but it wasn't too bad where I was walking. He kept on screaming as I walked. I was pretty close to him when he finally stopped yelling and reached over the long bar he was gripping, I think to turn the snowblower off. I was within range though, so I hit him on the head before he could do anything.

I hadn't hit him hard enough to do more than daze him—especially with that warm hat he was wearing. He turned to face me. The anger that had been on his face just before had turned to shock and his mouth was flapping open and closed like a pair of fish lips. I'd never seen a look like that on his face before. The wind charged again and blew into my face. I raised the shovel. He froze for a moment. And strangely, so did I. We were caught in this awful pause. This waiting.

It was excruciating.

Then, thank the gods, I took control of my muscles again and lowered the shovel another time. Not hard enough to do much. But it scared him so that he slid off the seat to the other side of the snowblower. I followed him around the roaring machine, forcing him to back out of the cleared path. He could choose between facing me and the shovel or the piles of snow. He chose the snow.

Oh, the snow. The wind, the cold, and the precipitation come together and leave behind these twisted drifts. Amazing enough in daylight, but in these mixed shadows of an early winter morning, on the edges of the reach of an electric bulb, they were otherworldly. A thousand years and I wouldn't see anything come close.

Dad only made it a few steps before the snow tripped him up. He fell. He was on his hands and knees. He was breathing in visible gasps. He screamed out something, but I couldn't make out the words. He started to rock back onto his feet in order to stand up, but I caught up with him and whacked him on the back. Not too hard, mind.

There was a sound like someone had said "hmph," then no sound at all. We went on pause again. This time it wasn't so terrible. For me, it was hopeful. But in a burst he rose to his hands and knees and then was up on his feet. His breathing now was wild, like an asthmatic's, and I could hear it through the noise of the blower.

He took two steps and looked back at me. I followed. He kept on, deeper into the drifts. It was a chase now. It was hard going in the snow. He went toward the fence, into the deepest part of the drift. I think he was planning to climb over the fence.

The snow. It was brand new. There hadn't been time for it to become packed. He had to break through it. I followed easily in the path he made, not rushing, taking my time, waiting. He began to bend over as he pushed into the snow, frantically swiping away the top layer to make way. It was as though he was swimming, and looking back now, I think I could say it was like he drowned in the snow.

Anyway, he gets close to the fence, real close, when he staggers and falls back into the snow behind. He lays there quiet like and I know it will all be okay.

I put the shovel back by the door. I took off my boots, shook the snow off onto the steps outside. Then I dried them, slow and careful. Hung up my coat, watching myself because I was pretty tired and could mess up easily. Slow and easy. Careful. Get back to my room and change into my pyjamas. Old sweatshirt, plaid flannel bottoms. Years old, but still comfy.

I got in bed and went to sleep, finally.

past tenses

CARRIE-JANE WILLIAMS

There'd been other park benches, of course, other Januaries.

There'd been benches that buckled beneath the weight of crushing confessions, and others that delighted in drips of ice cream and innocence.

There'd been decades of nondescript Januaries cowering in the creases of interminable winters.

This particular park bench, entangled in an organized mess of grammar and recollections, carved with the sharpest tools of forgiveness, has perhaps collected too much baggage to continue playing host. In its seemingly imminent retirement, the bench's wooden slats on iron feet emit the empathetic energy of an art installation, with all the sorrow and loneliness that visual vacancy evokes.

This particular January, unremarkable but for its seemingly purposeless plot twist, begs to go unnoticed, to lie as flat and forgotten as the resolutions that ease the calendar into new beginnings. Ideally, it would be the type of month that makes a person wonder where the time went—and not allow them to remember.

"Go ahead, Madame Claire Voyante," she said, laying a ten-dollar bill beside her champagne glass. "Tell me my future." Grace winked at a colleague sitting to her right, each of them facing a fortune teller.

Her interlocutor's smoky eyes widened in urgent, unblinking exaggeration.

"I hear many languages around you, my dear. I see that you have travelled."

"Madame Claire, you know I work for an international NGO; you're going to have to do better than that." She grabbed a corner of her purple bill and playfully tugged it back towards herself, the black satin mouth of her clutch open and containing a small stack of money destined for charity.

The chandeliers overhead sent diamonds dancing across the crystal ball between them and made the silver threads in Madame Claire's mauve headscarf sparkle like tree tinsel.

Inhaling deeply enough through her nose to make her back arch, Madame performed a dramatic closed-eyed sweep of her hands over the crystal ball and demanded, "Who was born in March, my dear?"

"Well, just about everybody, Madame. What else you got?"

"I sense an evasive Pisces, my dear. The one who got away. He will soon swim back to you and you must know that your love is eternal! But beware. You mustn't look to change your destiny!"

A familiar voice to Grace's left leaned conveniently towards her and she felt champagne bubbles tour jeté across her chest, bursting into a reckless confetti of oxytocin.

"That pesky Pisces who melted your stone-cold heart, hey, Scorpio? Tough as nails, she is, but much more than meets the eye, Madame Claire Voyante, let me tell you. She's also going to join me for lunch at her favourite hole-in-the-wall tomorrow. Twelve-thirty. Don't be late!" He turned towards his fortune teller with a grin and rubbed his hands together with the expectant determination of a dice toss.

Grace stood up, her undecorated hands smoothing out her black dress, eyes downcast, lips upturned. "Thank you, Madame Claire, for your time."

January eleventh.

One and one make eleven.

One plus one also makes two.

"One *dolsot bibimbap*, no egg, for the powerhouse, please, and I'll have the *bulgogi*." He gave her boot a gentle kick under the table.

In French, there's a past tense called the *passé composé*. It is called the *passé composé* because it is composed of two units, the auxiliary and the participle, just like eleven, and just like them.

Aaron smiled from the corner of his mouth and pulled a dried chickpea from the pocket of his hoodie. This chickpea, now casually resting beside metal chopsticks in a Korean restaurant, had travelled halfway across the world.

He picked it up and gently flicked it across the table to hit Grace between the eyes. "I'm still finding these things!" He dared not disclose that he'd collected a handful of them and carried one with him like a security blanket at all times.

They both laughed as they recalled "that time in Bamako" when Grace wanted to make a chickpea curry but tripped and sent the chickpeas scattering across the common kitchen like a hundred pearls from busted strings.

There was also the time they joined the mile-high club and immediately admitted it had no business being on their bucket list, and the time in university when they were partnered up for an impromptu exercise in simultaneous interpretation and she slipped unexpected vulgarities into a monologue about disenfranchised women in the health-care system just to throw him off and watch him stumble.

In French, the *passé composé* is the past tense dedicated to completed actions, actions that are done, finished, over.

This bench, settled upon during a post-lunch walk in the park, gave him space to hold her, for her to fall into him, for them both to go home. It gave him time to kiss her hair and for her fingers to seek warmth and shelter beneath the cuffs of his sleeves.

"We were so happy then. *Quand on s'aimait beaucoup.*" He swallowed.

The *imparfait*, or the imperfect: a tense used, in this case, to suggest that what was true in the past is no longer true.

When we really loved each other.

What was not imperfect was the prickly feeling of his beard beneath her fingernails as she caressed his face on the park bench, her cheek against his, the weight of words in their eyes.

The *imparfait* can be employed to express the equivalent of the English "used to."

They used to go to karaoke on Friday nights. He would pick her up religiously at six and if they were in N'Djamena or Kigali, say, and didn't know where to go, they would find bad karaoke online and sing together in their hotel rooms with the lights dimmed. If they weren't in the same city, a well-planned recording would usually be transmitted right on schedule.

He used to call her to say "You're the love of my life," then remind her that she, despite her heart of stone, was the one to say it first.

They used to fall asleep in each other's arms.

"Will I see you again?" Her question was tentative.

"Right here in this very spot. Wednesday at twelve-thirty. Don't be late."

The *imparfait* is many things, one of them being what, in English, is the past progressive, used to describe an action that was in progress in the past, not to imply that the past would progress. In English, the past progressive is also composed of two parts. Other than the gerund, which is a noun form, there is no "i-n-g" without the verb "to be."

She was wearing her prettiest outfit beneath her winter layers. She was waiting.

He was sitting at his computer working on a translation, conscious of the time.

She was holding a beach rock in her coat pocket. It reminded her of broken Japanese ceramic bowls, their cracks filled with gold. *Kintsukuroi*—a concept they both admired, the idea that objects, like people, are richer and more beautiful when they have stories and imperfections, when they have a past. She would press it into his palm. He would see the gold lines going through the rock that reminded her of him when she spotted it on the east coast and know exactly what it meant.

He was shutting off his phone, staring at a blinking cursor on his computer screen.

She was giving up, leaving, walking over the kind of snow that's formed after freezing rain: thin sheet ice on top and dense powder beneath the surface. The snow was cracking, wailing, and catching her fall with every step and she was mentally repairing the cracks she'd made with gold.

Le *plus-que-parfait*, the more-than-perfect, is the same as the past perfect in English. It is often partnered with the conditional.

If they had gotten trauma counselling after what they'd witnessed on their final overseas post, they wouldn't have drifted apart.

If he hadn't ignored her calls every time she tried to reach out, they could have made it work.

If she hadn't agreed to meet him on Monday, these feelings would still be repressed and everything would be okay.

If he had revealed that he had moved on with someone new, this wouldn't be happening right now.

It is a pointless exercise, not grammatically, but perhaps emotionally, to impose conditions on something that is alive and unconditional despite what sets it in a composed, imperfect, more-than-perfect past. But ultimately, there will be more park benches.

There will be more Januaries.

sugar

ALLISON GRAVES

My blood sugar was so high that winter that my doctor told me I really had to watch it. I told him I was buying a lot of those little bags of candy that you could get at Needs or Halliday's just right by the front counter. I tried to convince him they were hard to avoid buying and he said I needed to try harder.

The night after my doctor's appointment, my boyfriend and I watched *The Shining* in my bed. I had rearranged my room the week before and everything still felt out of order or something.

"Do you think it's better this way?"

"I don't know, I feel like we had a lot of nice memories when your room was organized the other way and now those memories feel, like, further away or something." Jacob said this as he finished a handful of Spicy Nacho Doritos. I kept looking at his hand every time it would leave the bag, waiting for him to wipe nacho dust onto my primary-coloured IKEA bedspread that I ordered last month.

"I think that's ridiculous. The memories just happened over there on that wall instead of this one." I pointed my finger straight out to the opposing wall and Jacob grabbed my finger and rolled on top of me. He kissed me and his breath tasted like nachos.

"Dude, Danny is riding that toy car on the big carpets, you love this part!"

Jacob kissed my cheek and rolled off me and said, "You're right. This part is the best."

We watched the rest of the movie in the dark and I could hear my roommates in the kitchen padding around in a way that made my heart feel full. My roommate Helen had started baking specialty cakes for people in St. John's and she was blowing up. People were hiring her to make their wedding cakes and their birthday cakes and cakes for office parties and retirement parties. Helen had started ordering piping tips of different sizes and designs on Amazon and they would come in really tiny packages in the mail every week, and every time one arrived it would make her happy.

There was a knock on my bedroom door. It was Helen. "Do you guys want a slice of cake?" she yelled through the door.

"Come in!"

Helen opened the door and on a tiny plate rimmed with flowers there was a slice of a cake with pink icing that she was making for a christening that weekend.

"They cancelled the christening," Helen said. "I guess they changed their mind and they don't want to baptize the baby? I don't know, Christianity seems wild to me." She had icing on her cheek and her hair was tied in a bun on top of her head.

"You look nice," I told her. Jacob nodded his head and hummed while he picked up the cake and took a bite. There was something so unselfconscious about Helen when she was working that I thought suited her. It was one of the only times that she wasn't in her head and overthinking everything.

"How was *The Shining*?"

"It was good," Jacob said. Jacob was taking an advanced film seminar at MUN about the cinematography of Stanley Kubrick and he was making me watch all of Kubrick's hits. Last week was *Eyes Wide Shut* and next week is *2001*.

"I don't know dude," I interrupted. "Kubrick seems wacky, like don't you think this movie is just supposed to be a warning against the American nuclear family or whatever. And how like you're going to die probably if you try to imitate that tradition cause it's ultimately just, like, bullshit."

Jacob took another bite of the cake and offered me the plate. I reminded him that my doctor told me I had to watch my sugar consumption and so he finished the slice.

"I think you're creating a narrative that's not there about all this nuclear family stuff," he said with his mouth full.

Helen had left the room and I could hear her humming in the kitchen.

"Well if it's not a warning against that it's sure as hell a warning against men who like have creative ambitions or like any sort of power in the family structure. Don't you think?"

Jacob laughed and said, "All work and no play makes Jacob a dull boy," and then he kissed me and his mouth tasted like cake.

A week later, a girl I used to work with at the Keg when I was sixteen, Carla, started advertising on her Facebook page that she was sugaring out of her house in Paradise. Sugaring was apparently this new way of waxing that everyone was talking about. I called her on a phone number I had saved from ages ago and told her I wanted to book an appointment for a Brazilian. Jacob thought I was being ridiculous but I told him I wanted to see what all the fuss was about. I took the bus up Kenmount

Road all the way and then walked the rest.

Carla answered the door and she looked the exact same except she had a deep wrinkle in the middle of her forehead and a vertical wrinkle between her eyes. She hugged me and it felt nice. She told me to go into her bathroom and change and wipe between my legs with stacked facecloths she had on the counter that were all different colours. She stepped behind a white curtain and waited for me to let her know when I was lying on the bed she had set up in her living room. The TV beside me was on CNN. Donald Trump had shut down the government and wouldn't reopen it until he had his wall built at the border. I felt relaxed by CNN. Like it was just noise that didn't make any sense and trying to make sense of it was pointless. Carla stuck her hand into a vat of a substance that was essentially honey and used this ball of honey to remove all the hair from my vagina. She kept on telling me I was doing well, as if I was accomplishing something big.

"So what are you even up to these days?"

I took a long breath through my nose and held the skin on my stomach, waiting for the next rip of hair. "Um, I'm working on a manuscript for my master's degree," I said, finishing the sentence quickly so I could prepare for the pain.

"Oh yeah, what are you writing about?"

"Um, I guess just like some modern short stories about like technology and Instagram and feeling empty and shit like that." Trying to articulate what I was doing seemed so sad to me in that moment.

Carla ripped the hair out of my flesh. "You're doing really well," she said again.

"Thank you," I replied and I felt a tear leak out of my left eye and down the side of my face.

After it was done, my crotch was sticky and sore. I went back to the bathroom and changed back into the Levi's I had bought at Value Village the week before. Carla was in the living room, on the other side of the curtain. She thanked me for supporting her new business endeavour and I thanked her for supporting me too. She gave me purple exfoliating gloves that I put in my pocket and I told her I would fulfill her aftercare regimen. She hugged me again and wished me good luck with my book. I gave her the fifty-dollar bill my father had gifted me for Christmas and a tip and I started walking through Paradise to the bus stop. Walking felt weird and my pants were irritating my crotch where it was sugared. I climbed a snowbank outside Carla's house to avoid a patch of ice and fell anyway. After I got up and started walking again, I started to cry uncontrollably in a way that felt so involuntary it was almost a betrayal. It had started getting dark at four in the afternoon in St. John's and this year—more than ever—I found it depressing and heavy. I missed the sun and I missed feeling okay.

I called Jacob and he answered on the third ring.

"What are you doing?" I said between sobs.

"I'm watching *Eyes Wide Shut* again. Do you think it's all supposed to be a dream?"

"I don't know . . . uh maybe."

"Hey, what's wrong?"

"I don't know, I feel so sad. That whole experience made me feel sad. I just feel like I always thought I was doing this really important work with my writing and I thought I had this big and sparkly future with it, but really I haven't even done anything since I stopped working at the Keg with this girl when I was sixteen and I just feel like all these things I thought about myself or these narratives are just like things I tell myself so I can feel okay but they're not actually based on any kind of truth."

I finished speaking and could see my breath in front of my face like fog. "And it's so fucking cold out and now I don't have any pubic hair."

"Do you want me to come get you? My mom said I can borrow the Jetta while they're in Florida."

"Okay. I'm going to walk to Chapters and maybe you'll pick me up there?"

"Okay. Don't freak out too much. You scare me when you're insecure. I don't like it."

When Jacob and I got home, all the lights were off and Helen had cupcakes on the table with a pink Post-it attached that said *Eat Me!* So I sat down on the counter and ate six.

"I think you're just feeling all these assurances around you dissolving," Jacob said. He was sitting on the floor with his back against the counter. "And it's not one thing in particular. But then you start to feel like all these things you're attached to will fulfill your desires for this like full life when in fact they probably won't."

"Isn't that so depressing though, like why do we attach ourselves to things if they don't make our lives better?"

"I don't know. I don't know anything."

By the time Helen got home all the cupcakes were gone and even though I felt empty, I felt full.

ten frames forever

ELIZABETH HICKS

"Paradise is nothing. I commute an hour past your house every day. I already said I would drive you home."

"I could stay."

"I know that's the last thing you want to do," I say.

"You're right," Frankie says.

It's an early December blizzard that hits while we're jamming at Rhiannon's. We aren't officially a band, but we're playing a show next Friday: Rhiannon, Frankie, and me. Frankie was a friend of a friend and now she's my friend, for real. She's singing for us. On Friday.

Heavy snow beginning Monday evening. It seems the gods were waiting for the six o'clock buzzer to release the storm, like confetti at the Super Bowl. My mother texts to warn me at seven: *I hope you're not driving tonight.* We emerge from the soundproof cave that is Rhiannon's basement to find the world has turned white in a short hour.

The neighbour calls, asking Rhiannon if I could please move my car so they can park outside their house tonight. They don't want to have to trudge a hundred metres up the road to shovel out their car the next morning.

We decide to end the jam early. A drive to Paradise in a storm like this will only get more difficult the longer we wait. Rhiannon waves at us through her steamy living room window.

Frankie and I are alone in my car, again. We have something to talk about, I think—something that should be addressed for the sake of her boyfriend and my sanity—but we haven't got to it yet. I tell her I'm going to drive slow, to be safe. I want to get her home but I also want her to never leave my car.

We're in a strange place. She has a long-term boyfriend. Rob. I drive her around a lot because she doesn't have a car or a driver's licence. The trouble (my trouble) began when she started getting touchy and I was touchy back and then I started questioning whether we were friends or what. We find excuses to see each other every Friday for what we've called *Friday Night Fun Club*. We had been for drives that were much too long and I wonder if I read too much into it. Sit at home and overanalyze everything she says to me. Does to me. I had felt this a few times before but never like I did with Frankie.

I spin the car around on Hamilton and soon I find myself wishing someone else were driving.

I am a nervous driver. I haven't explicitly told Frankie that but she knows. She has commented a few times on my slip-ups—a red light turned green during a too-long glance at my phone, a near-miss of a pedestrian on a crosswalk.

The paint was faded on that crosswalk. In fact, it was practically invisible on the right side. It wasn't a zebra crosswalk, either. It was the kind with just two white lines going perpendicular to the road, like a border of where a zebra crosswalk should be.

I rolled up over the crest of this hill and turned to check for oncoming cars. At the same time, Frankie squeaked something like "watch out" but she was too quiet and it was too late anyway. I had stopped directly on top of the crosswalk. There, on the left about two feet from my car, looking straight into my eyes with indisputable rage, was a woman in her late thirties with a baby strapped to her front. Her husband was behind her pushing a stroller with another kid.

It was an accident. And I didn't actually hit her. This lady started freaking out at me, crossed in front of my car, screamed at me like I had her baby tied to a spit and was actively roasting it over a campfire.

I just mouthed "sorry" over and over. Frankie tried not to make eye contact. The husband did the same. After a few moments I looked away but I still heard her screaming at me. She probably did more damage to that baby's eardrums than I could've done with the car.

Here, people walk out in front of your car all the time. Pedestrians have unconditional (but unofficial) right of way. Perhaps I shouldn't blame my almost killing of that lady and her baby on the fact that there was no crosswalk painted on the road. I should've expected them.

I will admit I find it difficult to interpret the enormous field of perception available when one is driving a vehicle. There are windows on every side. You, the driver, are at the centre of a sphere of liability. And there are mirrors, too, just in case you thought you could get away with looking in only one direction at a time. Don't forget, even for a second: you are responsible for every possible angle. You've gotta look outside, inside, adjust the radio, oh, the window is steaming up. We need air. Hot, cold, stop, start.

My Toyota Echo doesn't have the luxury of features like cruise control, so I'm truly alone out there, using my feet and my arms and my eyes all at the same time like I'm part of the machine. This chaos is why I don't drive a standard.

"Multi-tasking is what makes us human," Frankie says. "All kinds of thoughts at the same time. That's why dogs don't drive cars."

"I don't think that's the particular reason why dogs don't drive cars," I say.

"I'd say they will in, like, fifty years."

"It's the robots that are advancing. Not dogs."

"You can't know that, Bea."

"Dogs probably won't exist in fifty years."

"Mine will. Cocoa and Skylar are going to live forever. Or at least until I die."

"Will cats be driving cars too, then?" I ask.

"Probably. Cats are the kind of drivers that give you the finger after they cut you off. Insult to injury. Or the threat of injury, at least. Remember when you almost hit that baby on the crosswalk?"

"I thought we were going to let that rest." I want to tell her that I'm going to make sure she's safe with me.

"Nah," she says. "Gotta keep you on your toes."

"I'm on edge already."

"I thought you said you were comfortable with driving me home?"

"I am. I was kidding."

"Okay. Because you didn't have to."

I clock that we've been driving for about the amount of time it would normally take me to drive to her house from Rhiannon's and then back to mine. I appreciate the extra time. Heat flows from the dash. It's too hot in the car, but I need to keep the air on so the windows don't fog over. Frankie unzips her coat. I hesitate, then make a laborious attempt to take off mine. Frankie pulls on my sleeve so I can get my arm out while I steer with my other hand. She holds the wheel while I awkwardly wiggle out and tuck the large, puffy jacket around my hips. I am free but even sweatier than before.

We're quiet for a few minutes. Campus radio on low volume fills the silence. Frankie comments on the guy in a tiny truck with his back wheels slipping back and forth in front of us. The utter lack of traction reminds me of rubbing bleach between your fingers for a few seconds. Stop before it eats through the skin.

"He's taking a chance, going out in weather like this with no snow tires."

"I'm gonna hang back."

I let the truck fishtail away from us until it disappears into the wall of flurries ahead.

"Sometimes I question why I live here," Frankie says.

"I think we all do." I tug at my turtleneck. It feels tight and damp on my neck. "Why did you move here, anyway? I don't think I ever asked you that."

"Well, Rob's from here."

"Oh yeah, I think I knew that."

"His father died. A few years ago. So we came back to help take care of Rob's mom."

"Oh. I'm sorry."

"It's okay. I'm fine talking about it."

Frankie tells me about Rob and his mother. About how she lives in a home now and things are easier and more difficult at the same time.

"We drop in to visit her still. But no one says much." Frankie pauses. "The home has some nice outdoor space."

"That's good. That's . . . that's important," I say.

"It is. I'm glad. It's all weird, though. I'm sort of . . . not sure why we're here if it's not to take care of her. You know?"

I don't know, really. I hadn't ever had to take care of someone before.

"I'm sorry I didn't know this about you."

"Well, we did only meet last spring," she says.

"I guess so. Feels like longer."

I feel terrible then for thinking there is anything happening between Frankie and me. I am glad to be driving, too, so I have something to occupy my eyes and my hands and my brain. With Frankie, I felt I had finally grabbed onto something stable and real. That feeling fades as quickly as it arrived.

We near the commercial strip of Topsail Road and yellowy streetlights illuminate our view. I can see about a hundred metres in front of the car. A vast improvement over my previous near blindness.

"Is that a kid?" Frankie asks.

My grip immediately tightens on the wheel and my eyes scan. At the edge of our field of vision, a figure fights the wind. Holding onto backpack straps and kicking through what is already about ten centimetres of snow, this small person meanders into the four-lane road without a glance back at upcoming traffic.

"Sort of looks like it," I say. I feel a pang in my gut.

"Maybe we should pull over."

"Are you sure it's a kid?"

"Yes, yes, pull over."

It's a small city but a city nonetheless. I don't want to be accused of abducting a child. But it would be cruel to leave a child to walk home in this weather.

I listen to Frankie and stop the car beside our new friend.

Frankie rolls down her window. Winter air invades the car.

She is small enough to be a child. She is, however, a woman of about forty with thick black eyeliner and a scabbed face. Her unzipped red plaid winter jacket with faux fur trim clashes awfully with her purply plaid backpack. I glance at my own navy leather backpack in the back seat. A gift from my sister while she was in Prague. Frankie's is sitting next to mine. Soft and black with a pink furry pompom clipped to the zipper pull. I feel an urge to click the locks. Frankie zips her jacket back up to her chin.

"Hi. Are you, uh . . . okay?" Frankie asks.

"Yeah, yeah, I'm good," our new friend says.

She is obviously high. And also obviously freezing. The longer I look at her face the more I want to keep driving. I feel bad about that.

"Where are you going?" Frankie says.

I let my foot off the brake just a tiny bit.

"I was going to catch a bus at the mall. Could I get a ride to the Village?"

I point to the Village Mall's bright white-and-blue sign.

"It's right across the road."

"Oh. Yeah. Are you guys going Mount Carson way though?"

We are. Frankie opens her mouth but I lie before she has a chance to say anything. Our friend doesn't seem too concerned. I release the brake completely and the car slips away.

Frankie tells me she's sorry for making me stop. And for almost offering that person a ride. She panicked. I tell her that I didn't know what to do either. It's cold.

I look in the rear-view mirror and the woman has successfully made it across the road. She and the mall sink into whiteness.

Turning left, I change routes to avoid an especially steep hill. I am not sure if we will make it, even with studs.

"Are you gonna murder me?" Frankie asks.

"Not this time."

"I like this way better anyway. More of a view." She smiles and taps on the glass. It is caked with snow.

I'm dreading dropping her off.

She fixes her tangled hair. It's fine and blondish and twists perfectly into a bun with an expert turn of a scrunchie. I feel the weight of my single braid hanging like a rope down my back. I tell her I wish my hair was like hers.

"Bea, no. You have such nice hair. There's so much of it."

"It's no longer than yours."

"It's thick, though. I'm practically bald."

Her little cinnamon roll of a hairstyle squats on her head, refuting that claim. She sticks the zipper pull of her coat in her mouth and chews on it.

A pinkish purple glow fades into view. It catches me off guard. I rack my brain for a few seconds, but I can't come up with a possible source more logical than aliens.

"What is that?"

"It's St. Paul's," Frankie responds. "They got a new sign."

"Holy shit." I veer into the parking lot and there it is, in all its neon glory:

ST. PAUL'S

BOWLING LANES AND LEAGUE

Beneath, a blue bowling ball is on fire. The flames lick fuchsia up around the words. The ball looks like a face with two surprised eyes and mouth screaming "Oooo!"

"That must've cost thousands of dollars," I say.

"Don't you think it's worth it? It's incredible."

"It got us into the parking lot. Must be worth something. Think they're open?"

Out of the car, the storm doesn't feel as threatening. My feet feel sturdy on the ground. The warehouse-sized bowling alley shields us from the wind. I stare up at the sign and the tiny snowflakes sting my eyeballs.

Frankie tries the door and it's open. A rectangle of bluish light washes onto the parking lot.

"Come on. We're out in it anyway. And it is Friday Night Fun Club," she says.

I can't deny it.

A sign tells us to pay for a lane rental at the counter. Behind it are shelves and shelves of funky bowling shoes with little circles on the heels: 7, 7.5, 8, 8.5, 9 ... Across from them are Bud Light coolers. A couple of lonely Coors lurk on the bottom shelf.

There is a collage of grainy security screen grabs printed out and Scotch-taped to the side of the first cooler. It is titled *Wall of Fame: Do Not Serve.*

The group of banned patrons is small. Five of six of the photos show men in hoodies and/or ball caps, heads turned away as if they are avoiding the paparazzi. In the last photo, though, the culprit is a woman. She stares straight into the camera, grinning.

"It's our friend," Frankie notes. The Village Mall woman's unmistakable plaid backpack hangs from the crook of her elbow. For a short moment, I feel guilty again.

"Is she following us or something?" I joke, but when I look back at her photo, I swear I see her nod slightly.

I ring a bell but no one arrives. I tap my nails on the counter. Ring again. Nobody. I call out a loud hello.

If it weren't for the lights behind the counter and in the porch, St. Paul's Bowling Lanes and League would seem abandoned.

The only sound is the uneven buzz of the beer coolers.

"They went home early because of the storm and forgot to lock the door. These lights are never turned off. That's my guess," I say.

I hear Frankie's sharp inhale before she speaks.

"Unreal." She lets the vowel sounds drag. I know her plan.

Beyond the counter, where the lanes begin, is blackness. She saunters into it with carefree yet gentle steps.

I pop up myself up onto the counter and swing my legs over. I manage to kick a plastic cup labelled TIPS OR ELSE and send quarters, nickels, and dimes onto the floor.

"Careful!" Frankie calls. "Grab me a beer, will ya?"

A tiny key for the beer cooler hangs innocently next to its lock. I grab two beer and two pairs of shoes, and I flick three switches beneath a strip of masking tape that reads LANES in blue marker.

St. Paul's comes to life. Frankie gives an AHA! and I swing back over the counter with shoes under my arm and Bud Light in my hands.

The alley is a truly immaculate display. It's much too big for this city, with at least thirty freshly waxed wooden lanes sprawling down the warehouse. Racing down the lanes are bright lines of neon light—purple, pink, blue—suspended from a black ceiling. It's difficult to tell how high it is. The low-hanging hazy light makes the darkness beyond seem endless.

The machinery awakens with a hum and sends bowling balls flying down the underground tunnels toward us. Pearly and multicoloured, they arrive one by one with a whack, whack, whack.

"So much for being sneaky, huh?" I say. I stick my fingers into the three holes, lift with my knees, and send the ball straight into the gutter.

"That one was a warm-up," Frankie offers. She keys my initials into the scoring system and steps into the next lane. BV appears in a solitary row on the screen above my head.

"What, you're not going to play with me?" I ask.

"There's so many lanes here! I'm taking my own!" she says. Her screen blinks on: FQ. "We're still gonna compare scores. Don't worry. You're not getting off that easy."

We send ball after ball down our lanes and sweat starts to seep through the underarms of my black turtleneck. I tell Frankie what a relief it is to throw all my energy into something tangible and watch it take effect. Ball to pins. She tells me she feels like she's at Disneyland—like she's a kid having a blast on Space Mountain with no troubles in the world.

"But there's no snow in California," I say.

"It's a climate crisis, Bea. Anything could happen," Frankie says. "Besides, there's no snow in here, either."

"You're right, it's exactly like Disneyland," I say as I watch her massage the tendons in her right hand. I crack my knuckles. "St. Paul's should put that on the sign."

I'm counting the frames, but she doesn't seem aware of the scoreboard. I am winning by forty-five points when we reach the tenth frame.

"We get an extra one now, right?" Frankie asks, like I know something about bowling.

When her third ball tips into the gutter, her screen blinks but does not reset. She shrugs at me and sends another ball down the lane.

I take my turn in the tenth frame and it does the same.

For a second, my breath catches. I look down at my borrowed bowling shoes and dig my chin into my chest. The lack of closure incites a familiar anxiety. It's warm and I am aware again of my sweat-soaked pits. My face snaps up at the sound of Frankie's ball smashing into pins.

The game doesn't ever reset. It blinks every time in the tenth frame. No one working at St. Paul's Bowling Lanes and League ever shows up, and Frankie and I never leave.

We laugh and bowl and skate around in our slippery shoes. I tear the sleeves off my turtleneck, Frankie tightens her scrunchie, and eventually the heavy crack of bowling balls on the wooden floor sounds like nothing more than a tap on a car windowpane on a stormy night in December.

twilight airs, iron, water

TZU-HAO HSU

In the final weeks of his time on earth he rested in bed, partially reclined for comfort. He would sit a little straighter when his little Piglet, his first-born granddaughter, played the piano, savouring the delicate ringing throughout the house, seeing in his mind her hesitant, tiptoe touch grow confident as the familiarity of the tune took hold. The lullaby from his childhood.

She was piecing the melody together by ear and from memory. His soothing serenade to the once-fussy toddler came back to him first in shy, experimental stumbles, budding with daily practice into solid landings of chords and cadences, delivering the lyricism and dynamics of the song through her graceful, but oh-so-small hands. He gazed down at his own when she played, imagining himself still capable of the dexterity needed to make the instrument sing as she did, his thin, pale fingers painfully clawed, joints swollen and tight. Instead he conducted, his hands sailing through the air as the last notes rang and settled into purposeful, reverent silence. Then she would peer around the bedroom door, wondering if he approved of today's performance, which he always did.

He'd hand her some pocket change and ask her to pick up a meat bun from the street vendor just two houses down. *Grandma wouldn't let me have one, so this is our secret.* He winked and she grinned in response, the perfect partners in crime.

They would ride at first light to the market when he was healthy, sneaking out of the house like a couple of brigands. His wife and daughter did not approve of the grandchild waking so early but that never stopped them. She would perch on the back seat as he pedalled along on the bicycle in the cool air of the breaking dawn, the two of them chatting away to the frog songs in the rice paddies and the chimes of cicadas in the trees. They would carefully select from earth-fresh produce, find a couple of buttery, sweet sugar cookies for a snack later, and pick up soup and noodles for everyone in the house, returning just in time for a family breakfast.

She always sat on his left at the dining table. They would top up each other's bowls with their favourite foods while the family looked on, commenting on the unlikely bond between the old and young, watching them getting into trouble and nonsense in the name of education and adventure. She learned from him to dig for fresh bamboo shoots and catch frogs, and he learned not to underestimate how quickly a small child could ascend a mango tree in search of a ripe fruit.

In her dream she was casually dressed in jeans and a T-shirt, and he was very handsomely attired in a pair of tan trousers with a smart, buttoned-up shirt, a cream-coloured sweater with a navy-accented V-neck, a style he always favoured, and a cabbie hat to polish off the ensemble.

I'm quite upset with you. She was as haughty as ever and his lips curled, his eyes softening in that apologetic way.

I know. He nodded as he took the lead, strolling down the path paved with obsidian slate, framed by chest-high bushes dotted with pink buds. You have never needed my guidance and I was needed elsewhere.

It isn't about guidance, I just . . . I missed you terribly and thought I was your favourite. I know I was your favourite. She sounded sulky, almost two decades later and still very much the little girl that he left behind in life. Why didn't you ever visit me?

These things are beyond me and I can't be everywhere, unfortunately. I thought I did the right thing, but clearly I have let you down.

You haven't. You never ever did. I just wished you'd come to see me every once in a while, so I could let you know I was doing okay and you had nothing to worry about. Maybe you would have been proud of what I've done. I scored double gold in the music festival that year, and . . .

And first place in your essay competition, science fair, and became the volleyball team captain. I know. You couldn't see me, but it doesn't mean I wasn't looking.

. . . Well, it would still have been nice to know you were there. She shrank a little then, feeling sheepish for the misplaced hurt. Then, softly: It wasn't fair, you going so early.

Your mother says the same thing to me all the time, Piglet. The treasured childhood pet name brought a warmth she hadn't felt in years. But that is not for us to choose, unfortunately.

I know, and that's what makes life so amazing, blah blah blah, wisdom from the elder, and so on and so forth. She rolled her eyes and kicked a small rock. What is it like, where you are?

I can't tell you, but everyone you think belongs here is here. We are happy, and we miss you as much as you miss us.

She hadn't noticed the magic of her island in her youth, that lush, rich fragrance of twilight blossoms falling flat on an unappreciative little nose; she was interested only in the hunt for the berries on the neighbour's bushes or the savoury rice balls coming from the pedalling vendor's cart.

How quickly these things were taken away.

They said it was becoming a public safety hazard. Her uncle let out a derisive puff of vanilla-scented smoke. What they actually meant was they flattened another village to build a box-store shopping centre. Bah! These progressives just hate the old ways. Nobody will tell me these suppliers and vendors and big-worded important people can get me a taro or bamboo shoot as fresh as Chin's boy down the road, and for half the price, too! But the government wants to see a, what is it? Economic return on their investments. And street vendors are unsanitary now. They haven't been unsanitary for hundreds of years but suddenly nothing passes inspection. Then his eyes met hers. Is that what you study in school?

The night market she recalled fondly from her childhood had finally folded under the bureaucratic pressure to modernize, doing significant damage to the livelihood of many friends.

I—I don't support this type of development, she said. She'd faltered, fearing her education was somehow offensive to her beloved uncle.

I know you don't. He visibly relaxed, noting her discomfort on the subject. You of all the children always appreciated the importance of the old ways. He laid down his pipe and stretched, regret in his voice. I saw you looking for fireflies last night. I'm afraid they are all gone, my darling girl. I'm sure you noticed how quiet it is in the night now.

Yes. She did notice. The frogs have stopped singing.

She poured her uncle another cup of tea and said goodnight, then went out to the balcony in search of a breeze. A crescent moon, blurry with pollution, kept her company instead. Wrinkling her nose against the latest modified car to roar past the street, she watered the plants her grandfather loved, a lone hanging garden in a town infested by industrialization.

Why didn't you come home? She and her younger cousin sat arm in arm on their late grandfather's favourite bench, basking in the heat of the afternoon sun coming through the skylights in the cozy solarium. The canaries that used to belong to the dearly departed man chirped a tune, appreciative of the fresh fruits and water recently supplied by the two lounging women. They were close in age and had always been more like sisters than extended family.

Come where, and for what? she asked, knowing exactly what her cousin meant by the question.

His funeral. You were the only grandchild missing. The younger woman shrugged. We all know you were his favourite.

There was no jealousy or hurt in this conversation; nevertheless, their physical closeness now brought a level of discomfort.

I don't know, my parents kept me overseas. She shifted away slightly. It was really up to them, I guess.

It was weird not to see you. Even the littlest one, what's his name again? We never see him. He was there. He fell asleep halfway through the ceremony and my mom had to carry him away. Her cousin yawned, leaned into her shoulder, and sighed. Why didn't you come home?

Would it have made a difference? They stared at the old man's portrait on the opposite wall, the sepia glowing with his gentle dignity. I couldn't bring him back.

Nobody could, but you were special to him. She felt the slight tremble that was always a precursor to her cousin's tears and decided to stay still and quiet.

Do you miss him? the younger woman asked. I miss him so much. I still cry about him every once in a while.

He used to say boys were iron born and girls water made. She stroked her cousin's hair then, noting how tall she had become, and yet still so young. Are you water made? You're snotting a river there.

I am half and half. Her cousin laughed and blew a raspberry.

How about you? Are you all iron? Like that English lady? The prime minister? Is that what you learned from being in the West?

Her name was Thatcher. And no. She looked away then and the younger woman had the wisdom to simply envelop her in a hug. I'm a bit watery today.

The song came from Mommy's grandpa. Mommy would sit at the piano and move our fingers one by one to teach us the notes. She said great-grandpa always called her Piglet and that he loved the piano best. The notes didn't always sound right but we like it, and Mommy told the best stories whenever we played together. She promised she would tell us about a time when she fell asleep in a mango tree. Imagine, a mango tree!

But for now, the mango tree can wait. We came a very long way today to do something special. Mommy said this will be the best adventure and look, tricycles!

Everyone is here, you say? She mused. So . . . everyone?

Yes. My mah-jong table is finally complete. He laughed then. We are still here. Always here.

Thanks for taking me out for a walk. She felt the threat of tears and forced a laugh to fight it, feeling the warmth of the rising sun on her face. In my favourite garden, too.

The castle on the river. His smile was becoming hazier, the way dreams often do when wakefulness is about to set back in. We always said we'd come back.

Mom said you asked her to be your daughter again in your next life. She blurted it out then and was instantly embarrassed. I just want you to know, before I wake up, that I . . .

Yes, I would like to be your grandfather in our next life.

He held out his arms for a hug then. It had always, always been kindness, patience and all the things love is made of, in the charmed circle of his embrace.

Be well, my Piglet.

Is this how you remember it? he asked, strolling with her hand in his, just behind their excited little girls, heading down the newly established pedestrian zone.

Not quite. He could sense her nervousness, a mixture of joy and longing for a time that can never be again. But I am really glad we are here. I needed them to see this, to see where I came from.

It is quite beautiful. When your cousin said they were revitalizing the town I didn't think . . . given what the place looked like during our last visit. He nodded, appreciating the architectural genius that fostered more greenery and reintroduced waterways in a town all but claimed by steel, concrete, and neon lights. Is that a pond up ahead?

I think so . . . in the old rice paddies too. There was a spring to her steps as her walk gave way to a light jog, cleverly disguised as an attempt to catch up to the children, but he knew it to be excitement. I wonder, I wonder if . . .

The young ones began pedalling faster when their noses caught the scent of the soup and noodles, with a generous helping of buttery, sweet sugar cookies. The crowd parted for the twins on tricycles, welcoming the giddy laughter of children again in the old-now-new square.

She caught up to them when they stopped. And tilted their heads.

And listened.

starecase

BENJAMIN C. DUGDALE

Mom is doing that quiet laugh that only my uncles ever seem to get from her. The twin cigarettes' chimneys of Du Maurier haze coil into one single, foggy thing and then that joined thing floats out of the dining room and toward me through the kitchen's pass-through. Mom's tin cigarette case clasps shut with a satisfying click, as it always does. I can't find what I'm looking for in the junk drawer, but maybe a steak knife will do.

Middle-Uncle's come from the Quonset across the road to tell my mom about some prank him and Baby-Uncle are pulling on my father. They've hidden something inside Dad's combine cab. Middle-Uncle's coffee is snow-white, and his cigarette smoke is scratchy and hovering now, a greying storm cloud over the coffee's perfect egg-white mirror. He bangs his spoon three times on the cup, then sets it down right on the varnish of the table, just like he always does. My mom is trying hard to suppress some emotion, covering her mouth with her hand, her eyebrows arched the way only my mom could arch them, like a stretched elastic band waiting to snap. I think it's laughter, but she always looks worried when she laughs, and she laughs when she's worried sometimes too.

"I don't think he's going to take this well, Hank. I think you should go stop him from getting out into the field before he finds out." Middle-Uncle relates that Dad left the shop about an hour ago, as soon as they got the thresher running again, so there was no point in rushing out to rescue him now: "Damage is done. And maybe it naps all day. Maybe it died in the night. *Hoo* knows?" He holds his gut like the time Dad beat him up at the 4H cattle sale, when he said something about the heifers, or my sisters.

Mom frowns, smothers her cigarette, and drops her hand into her apron's pocket. She's surprised to find me in the kitchen, eyes me queerly, takes the steak knife away and sets it back into the plastic cutlery tray, but doesn't say anything rude to me. She checks on the chili supper she's cooking for everyone who's out in the field today; sounds like it's only ever Dad out there, given his brothers always coming over here, always telling Mom jokes. Maybe that guy from New Zealand who works for us who I can't understand very well, that hides stuff in Middle-Sister's roof, where the ceiling tiles slide aside; I'm not allowed to talk about that, sworn to secrecy, and by the only sacred act in this whole damn house, no less—the pinky-swear. Mom's strange inquiring gaze bothers me, but I think I know where it's coming from.

These days after school I usually go around the house in one of three shirts I like: two are identical long long long white Zellers T-shirts, with the mascot, Zeddy, languishing like a benzo'd trophy wife across a space-rocket; the heavy print is always stuck to itself when it comes out of the dryer. The third shirt I wear these days—I wish I had another, but my parents refuse to buy a second—is my Batman tee, black with the yellow puck with the black bat silhouette in it, which Dad had bought in an XL but found was a touch too tight and had been mad about for whatever reason; I for one thought it was cool the shirt was tight enough to show his herniated belly button nosing through the fabric; for those out of the loop, hernias are something only people who are realllly strong get.

Those are my three tees, my *tees three*, and that's all I *need*, though I'd kill for another Batman one. Sometimes the basement is so cold that I will put on underwear to go down there, but other days I'm braver, stick to the tee, to its simplicity.

It doesn't bother me that I'm the only person who walks around the house nearly naked, though my dad seems angry about it, well angry at my mom about it when he doesn't realize I can hear him—something about looking into the eyes of a six-year-old boy in nothing but an over-large Batman T-shirt that he himself used to own seems to neutralize Dad-mad opinions on boho fashion choices. I like how the shirt can be twirly when I choose to play girly to both sisters' applause, before or after I lip-sync to Seal's "Kiss from a Rose," on loudspeaker only in my mind.

Dad's belly doesn't let him show off his nice belts or buckles that he sometimes wears on weekends, and he usually leaves his dress shirts untucked, sticking out far enough from his pants that they cast a shadow; when he wears his pants high up and his shirt tucked in, he looks just like Doctor Robotnik, Sonic's nemesis, which is like a best friend but the other way; Kintobor was his name before he was evil, when he was Sonic's best friend; Dad doesn't like me calling him Robotnik, or Eggman either; I don't think he gets that Robotnik and Eggman (and, when you think about it, Kintobor too) are the same guy. I like that my twirly long shirt can cover everything and that I only sometimes don't shake enough after peeing and only sometimes leave a lugubrious piss droplet on its bottom-most trim. Only once have I caught my dad staring at the dark spot, but he didn't say anything about it within earshot.

Middle-Uncle finishes his smoke and is gone before its butt stops smouldering, his coffee mostly full and not poured out in the sink even. In short order Mom's out the door too, taking her smoke with her because "wasteful" isn't in her dictionary, and yelling to my sisters to make sure I eat something, and she'll be back soon enough. None of us say anything in response, each involved in our much more interesting world of boys or books or logs or a light hitting gloom on the grey.

At six years old, my logic is as follows: my wingspan lets me palm the walls bracketing the steps going from the landing to the second floor, and since I can master the passage this way, I claim dominion over this whole staircase. No one may come or go without my permission. Laundry embargo, everyone can frig off and leave me alone, because only I am guaranteed safe passage up these stairs. This site will do just fine for my purposes.

I am the smallest member of my family, though I suspect this is merely because I am the youngest, and I know I will eventually surpass Middle-Sister, and possibly even Oldest-Sister; it is hard to fathom ever approaching a size where I might mimic my dad's scuba-tank forearms, and my mom is so often hugging me that I can't visualize how wide her arms would go if they weren't always wrapped so tightly around someone, or mending something, or dicing something, and, and you know what, if her arms came undone from a hug I think they might go wide as the whole horizon! A terrifying thought. That's entirely too long.

I start slotting together the foundations for this Lincoln Log cabin, and the space shrinks so small, the same way you sometimes have to shrug your shoulders in to squeeze past someone in the busy aisles at Co-op. I don't feel big when I look at small things, I feel like I scale to them instead of the other way around. The aisle at Co-op I hate the most is the one with all that laundry stuff, because it gives me a headache, and it makes me feel small and spotty-eyed, but not small in a cool way, like the little Lincoln Logs do.

The steps are so plush, too soft for this Lincoln cabin to stand the test of time, so why is the rug on these steps so harsh when you slide down it on your bare bum; these steps are so so silent that I can't tell if Mom and Dad are ever gonna come up to tuck me in some nights, till suddenly they burst through my door in tandem and spook me; I hate this part of my day, every day, but last time I cried about it I got in trouble for it, or my mom did, and I heard it through the doorway.

I've been working all day on a troubling problem: how do you get a diagonal into this cabin? How do you cut the corner off? Don't get me wrong, I don't have a problem with squares. I'm sure there's a way to do this, though, but my dad didn't understand me when I asked him how to do it. I told him I want it to be like half a grilled cheese, and that I want it to go really high, like on TV.

"That's a skyscraper. That's not what those're for."

Why would I make a stupid cabin? Who lives in a cabin? We don't live in a cabin. Our house has a round part where the living room bulges out, like when you press carefully on one part of a balloon animal and it sticks out somewhere else. It's not round, though; I guess it's kind of like a stop sign, but the one window that broke in a storm last year just has a piece of plywood up there, because it's so expensive to make bent glass or something.

I haven't figured it out yet, but why would they make them so you can't do that? The logs, that is. Why do they have to come together at odds with each other, notched planes clasping together firm as the handshakes Dad's been trying to workshop with me.

"If it's soft I'm gonna squeeze you until it hurts, until you firm it up."

He steals points I miss when we play crib too, but we don't play that much while it's harvest, because as Baby-Uncle says, "That fat bastard's too tired to pull off his own socks the end the day, in't he, Wendy?"

Oldest-Sister kicks down my skyscraper when she blows by me crying, like a real idiot. I throw a few logs up the stairs after her but too slow, and I hear Middle-Sister's door mirror clink. I run up to survey the damage and the door's mirror is cracked with a shaky C-shape, or like when Oldest-Sister gets a tummy ache and hogs the hot water bottle, bent over. Yeah, like the mirror is bent over with "cramps." Catch-all BS excuse, you ask me. Oldest-Sister looks out with just one eye from her dark room, and seeing me see her, slams it shut. I'll blame Middle-Sister's mirror on Oldest-Sister, because she basically did it, and she does everything wrong these days, though it's kind of magic now, how the things in it all of a sudden bound when they cross the crack. I touch it, and it nips me, and I suck my finger and look at where it hurts. I blow on the cut, like I blow on the *Sonic 2* cartridge when it's not working, and a little see-through flap waves as I blow, but the interruption in the fingerprint gushes out new blood. Oldest-Sister comes out to use the bathroom and catches me before I can faint and fall.

"No peroxide."

"Yes peroxide."

"Leave me alone, you bitch."

But it's too late, and the fizz consumes my finger, and even when I throw the bottle at the tub, Oldest-Sister is keeping her cool. I tell her, "your eyes are red and stupid."

"What else is new?"

She has me there. She's almost as deft as me when it comes to these battles of wit, but not quite. If I hadn't just almost lost my whole finger, which she too-snugly bandages, and which immediately takes to itching, I wouldn't have let her win this argument.

Taking my silence, accurately, as capitulation, she pivots, tries to help calm me down. She re-caps the peroxide and starts the shower to rinse away the stench. Her voice big and frightening like Dad's from the smallness of the bathroom, she asks, "so, you know what it is they put in the combine cab?"

"I don't know what you're talking about."

"Sure you do. You were standing there, holding a knife like a weirdo, listening in on them."

"You must have me confused with someone else."

"I bet it's a bomb. He pushed them all too far this time. They're gonna get him back."

"Like the Penguin did to Batman. But Batman's sharp! Batman got rid of that one." My face hurts from the seatbelt snap of my improved mood, my perfect, be-toothed smile.

"The Penguin took *control* of the Batmobile, he didn't plant a bomb."

"Then why did those police cars blow up when he threw it away?"

"I don't think you're remembering that right."

Earlier this week Middle-Sister and I called a truce for about ten minutes to spy on Oldest-Sister helping Dad in the yard.

Dad's trying to get the backhoe going so that he can go fix the ditch at the neighbours', because something's stuck in there, interrupting their water somewhere along its ditch artery before it gets to their dugout.

"I bet it's a dead body." Middle-Sister speculates without emotion, her huge glasses making her look like twice the idiot I know she is.

"No, because bodies always wash up in *our* dugout, idiot. Read a book or something."

She laughs like I was telling a joke, which I wasn't, but I maintain the truce, as I am not a creature without dignity, without honour. We can tell Dad is swearing because Oldest-Sister is covering her ears, wearing Dad's baggy track jacket, floppy swooshy cuffs sprouting from her ears—"Or maybe it's just too cold," Middle-Sister mind-reads in reply to me. Dad has a can of ether he's spraying straight into the engine, and Oldest-Sister is using one hand now to point the flashlight at it, and her other one to try the key. It fires up, and an explosion comes straight from the engine and Dad's nothing but a silhouette for a second, and then the bucket plummets straight down into the driveway, a wound gouged into the yard gutter that is grass and gravel lane alike. We duck from the window as soon as Dad's silhouette rears in anger toward the house, before our eyes can adjust, but we can hear him take it out on Oldest-Sister—well, we *feel* it, even if we can't hear it.

The stairs to the basement from the ground floor are unfinished, of lesser quality than those that lead to our bedrooms on the second floor. A navy-blue cartoon tongue of frayed rug rolls over the tippity toppest step, a tongue tonguing around the curve and then down under and then along the flat plane a lickle, stapled flush about an inch above where it cowlicks up, where its fraying white whiskers cameo. If you want to take smelly markers to make something secret, you can always draw on the part where the rug quits, make a treasure map or try to do that one where you draw a cat without lifting up the marker even once in the middle of it; Oldest-Sister's guy friends do this, but they always show the cat's butt, which is pretty gross, even if it's funny. Other than that top step, the stairs are arid all the way down. Each step is alarm-loud, so when you come and go, everyone in the house can echolocate your exact position, like bats.

The whole basement is unfinished. I like to come down here because the cold of the concrete is so cold it makes my feet ache, ache deep like a stomach cramp, and what a wild feeling that is! It makes me feel alive, and sometimes I test myself to see just how long I can stand still before I have to run back up and have Mom rub my toes warm one by one, though I kicked her in the face last time she tried to gobble them up because it tickled, and she cried about it but lied about crying, even though I could see her crying right there in front of me; moms are allowed to lie, same as dads are allowed to yell.

When you get to the bottom of the basement steps and turn to the right there's the cold room, with the gooey heavy-metal deep-freeze buzz; in the cold room's back corner, the door to the furnace room doesn't close over properly, and it terrifies me that we have a door we cannot close in our midst, that we don't talk about it. The main berth of the basement is for the sofa, though formerly for the TV too. Since the Christmas arrival of a Sega Genesis last year, the TV lives upstairs in the dining room, and you can see it from the kitchen pass-through, like a window you don't need glass for; Mom seems to really like this pass-through that Dad took down a wall for last year, but he's never once said "you're welcome" to Mom despite her diligent daily thanks, smiling and crying, dicing onions and watching

Buck Shot and Benny through this architectural marvel, singing whispersoft along to "Sixteen Chickens and a Tambourine."

In this new Sega era, when you sit on the basement sofa, all there is to stare at is the plain back wall's load-bearing beams, beams partitioning itchy insulation; it seems the couch is just down there now for chilly meditation. My two sisters—seven and ten years older than me respectively—often kick me out of the basement when they have company, and once, Oldest-Sister has the balls to say I can only keep hanging out with her and the many drooling dudes around her if I put on "some friggin underwear already," but I won't be bullied by some mere girl, so I storm upstairs to play *Sonic 2* on the Sega TV set-up we've insinuated into the corner of the dining room and play until my vision's spotted by need-to-pee. I haven't deduced what it is about the basement's Pink Panther palette that makes the ultimate hang-out spot for sisters and their moody, lingering boyfriends, but I am sure my Batman-like detective skills will prove fruitful soon.

Sonic nyooms east forever and ever collecting golden rings, until he crashes into spikes or monsters, and then his whole existence flashes invisible-visible, invisible-visible, coins scattered east too. I play until they ask me not to anymore, and when I close my eyes I still see him going, until the fright of the gooey reverberation downstairs creeps into my meditation, and I start to speculate on whatever horrible thing those ungrateful uncles have hidden in Dad's combine.

The door for Middle-Sister's bedroom is straight ahead when you come to the second-floor landing. On its outside is the compromised body-length mirror, and sometimes I spook myself as I crest the top step, catch my own reflection bobbing closer and higher and bigger. I moved my Mickey Mouse pillow into Middle-Sister's room last week and was baffled to find her still using her room after I'd clearly claimed it with my Mickey pillow.

You see, I know I'm intelligent because Oldest-Sister really applauded when I explained that balloons shrink over time because the air inside them "disintegrates," clearly a combination of the words "disappear" and "integrates," the latter of which I don't have a total handle on yet, but enough to have figured out the portmanteau's etymology from. I know I'm intelligent because this balloon science is just one example of several things I've gotten raised eyebrows and *oh wow, I didn't know thats* for lately. She's been kind of terrible to me all the time this year, probably jealous I'm so much smarter than she is.

But my Mickey Mouse pillow didn't lay claim to Middle's bedroom, and I want the room now, and I am "the baby," and Middle has a room with a window with a view to the dugout I overheard a weird story about, from my grandma to my dad, about drowning some black cat, or some drowning black cat is what she said, maybe. Or did I dream that? Mom said I must have dreamt that up, but of course Dad said she's not the expert on nothin', and "especially not harvest," which sounds like a huge headache, and like something they should consider avoiding in the future, if it's really so much work for so little.

I'm not allowed to play out there by the dugout ever since our last dog drowned in it too, but that was different than the cat somehow.

"That was a good damn dog," Mom had said when I asked about it, her eyes somewhere else. I get it. My mind goes to other worlds all the time too. It's a smart-person thing.

Last month Middle-Sister's "boyfriend" took my Hush Puppy stuffy and hockey-boy threw it toward the dugout. Dad'd been mad at Mom about the snow and the frost on the ground this early in the year, because they haven't finished taking off the crop, but I'm not sure what Mom's got to do with that, unless, well, no, she couldn't possibly be a weather witch. *Unless.* Whatever the case, he was taking her for Edo Ichiban in the City, because he lost their whisper-yelly argument, I guess. Oldest-Sister was with the Burndreds at tae kwon do, but I bet I could still kick her ass.

    Intrepid, I ventured out in nothing but my shirt and some of my mom's slippers, which were all cronch cronch cronch, and when I got to the dugout's slope, I saw my Hush Puppy sitting upright on the ice forming along the mouth's inner lip. The moon was so bright that you could see it even before the sky was dark, even in the misty blue, and the moon's light was steady on the ice scabbed around the dugout's mouth but shimmering in the centre where it hadn't all frozen over. By the time I got back to the door I realized I'd lost Mom's left slipper somewhere on the way back, and my hands were so shaky I couldn't turn the handle, or maybe it was locked, Middle-Sister trying to get some of that privacy she claims no one in the house gives her. I went back to the dugout to get the slipper, looking at the dent the puppy left on its icy lip, flaking like my nose when I have to blow it too much, all white and sore, and I wondered if the dog we had when I was little, so little I don't remember, I wonder if she's down there still, and I wonder how I know it's a girl too, was a girl, I guess, because when you're dead you're not anything. And the door's still locked when I get back, if that's what it is and it's not just my hands that are so messed up already that I can't turn the handle, and I bang the door and scream until I get let back in, and I set my idle at T A N T R U M until Mom comes home an hour later and executes a wrath beyond my wildest hopes, so potent I almost start to feel bad for doomed Middle-Sister.

Middle thinks the thing the uncles left in Dad's combine this afternoon is bad. "It's a gun. You know? He doesn't let me see it either, but Kirk was telling me about it." Middle looks like

Ronald McDonald today, all that makeup, and her chest is all pushed together like there's a crease down her middle, and with her skeletal frame it looks less like cleavage and more like a manufacturing defect, or a car run head-on into and perfectly centred with the telephone pole, wrapped around like.

"What's with the makeup? Kirk said makeup's a trap, designed to waste your time and dupe unsuspecting boys."

"If only it worked that well!" Some weird bad shape sponge thing—obtuse maybe?—too big an angle, making her all ghostly now, corpse-paint for her cheekbones that stick out too far. She does that mind-read thing again, holds the sponge and a brush just like it up, and lectures: "It's a reflex angle. See?" Draws her finger across the handle, then around how the brush goes. "It supersedes 180 degrees."

"It's like that snake in that stupid scary movie you made me watch."

"Which?"

"It's named after a snake. That's all I got for you."

"I remember now. We weren't going to watch *Mortal Kombat* again, okay?"

"*Mortal Kombat: Annihilation*. And I voted for *Liar Liar*."

"Well you lost the vote."

"Voting's stupid."

"That's what Kirk thinks."

"So the makeup. You going out with someone? Better not be hockey nazi."

A many-toothed thing gums up and blackens her blonde eyelashes. Does the same thing to them as her bra does to her chest. Too conspicuous. She pivots again.

"Yeah, it's probably one of Dad's guns. Maybe they put a pink bow on it, like as a prank. Or maybe he had it in there, and then they replaced it with a SuperSoaker."

"How many guns does he have?"

"Hard to say. Kirk said it's at least a few. She's even held the one, she says."

"Liar."

"Liar liar, could be. So this is reflex, yes." She holds the sponge up again, suspiciously like Ms. PAC-MAN, like in Cousin's arcade cabinet, upstairs in the Quonset with the pool-table. She retrieves a brush from the filthy, loud pouch she keeps all her brushes and expensive pencil crayons in. "And this?"

"Straight angle. No degree."

"Zero degrees, right. And this?" Tugs up the sink-plug toggle, upright at the back of the tap's long, pitted neck.

"Right." I turn the tap on. Water starts to rise.

"Right indeed." She turns the taps off, and the water stays where it is. She travels to her room and I trail her.

"You really think a gun?"

"Yeah. Maybe it'll go off and shoot him in the foot when he least suspects it."

"I don't want him to get shot."

The unforgiving quick thwip of zipped shut pouch. "Okay, out. I've got to finish getting ready for J. D."

"I hate that hockey nazi."

"He didn't even make the team this year."

She slams her door shut, a little puff of space as her mirror parts from the door a second from the force. I look at the mirror a minute longer. I've thought lately how mirrors mess up everything. When I think of the world inside the mirror, outside our world, I wonder if the me on that side always breathes when I exhale. If they also get so worked up about breathing that they have to focus on it, that it won't happen automatically? Or if the opposite held true? And were they a boy or a girl on the outside? If I walked through that mirror, would I find brothers, or just kinder sisters? So strange, how "opposite" seems to pivot so many ways at once when you really look at it, that "difference" never clarifies things the way the world promises it oughta.

There's a show on sometimes called *The Odd See*, and in it a kid lives in two places too. The second season I got in an argument with my sisters, sure they'd recast the kid, but apparently it was still him, just grown up. So anyhoodle, idiot kid hits his head on a shopping cart or something, right? And so he ends up in a coma, but all the while, he's somewhere else too!

Why didn't my Mickey pillow get rid of Middle? I chew my shirt collar, my teeth meeting each other in the thin centre of the threadbare cotton. Does she not fathom that this is my most-prized possession? That I had to suffer the too-social Disneycation with the rest of them (plus many prissy cousins) to get this pillow, and that if it's in her room, then it must not be her room at all? I climb the steps to give her a piece of my mind, remind her what the middle kid deserves—an invisibility in the family hierarchy, a polite designation as forgotten versus an acute uncomfortable attention as too middling, not enough of any one or the other, and it is her choice which status she wants, but there'll be heck to pay if she doesn't surrender that bedroom and its window, or at least return my Mickey pillow—and as I realize the precipice, halfway out of breath, I'm already imagining our argument in my head, just how to make her shut up and listen to me already.

I don't catch myself in the mirror this time though, because the door is open inward, and in the mirror, Middle is naked, looking at herself, hands on her collarbone like she's miming "me Jane" to some intelligent animal, and she's naked in a private way, but really she's somehow not naked at all, some invisible and permanent change about her posture and body and everything, tight as an onion skin, her skeletal angles mending the mirror's fault, bringing two unlike things back together, smoothing the crease that forms her wicked features.

I look away from the foreground FUPA, cross-hatched with hair, to her marching-band Shako with its little feather muff lazing, hat hung on an angle I couldn't tell you the degrees of, hung from the vanity's soft-metal coat hook.

Dad yelled at her coach one day last summer, because coach was mad Middle's left arm was double-jointed, won't go flush to her side without baring her elbow-pit, or when she forced the elbow-pit in, the elbow itself sticking out into someone else's ribs. Dad was so much louder than that other guy, what a show. Better than whatever racket it is the "band" usually makes.

The screen door clatters downstairs, and I bound down to see Mom first, tell her who broke the mirror while she was out, and I am adroitly dodging scattered logs, moving with purpose and now with a vague understanding that I'm probably not supposed to see my sister naked, and unsure if she saw me see her when the screen door sounded below us, not that it matters because we still have baths together sometimes, but that it maybe matters now, like she is different now than before, abandoning me in the world I live in to go and join Oldest-Sister and the rest of them, leaving me with no one but the hush and the Hush Puppy stuffy, lousy with the mildew of never leaving my side from now until the day I die I swear to fucking god.

Dad's forearms log-drive through the foyer and then the rest of him too with a small red toolbox tucked football-tight to his belly, and he rushes to the dining room table without taking off his muddy boots. He's screaming "Ma, come help." There's something wrong with Dad's eyes, they're wet and red, like when he gets his recurring sty, but shinier. He flips the lock-latch up on the toolbox, and Middle-Sister suddenly behind me puts her housecoat arms on my shoulders, and Dad opens up the blood-red toolbox top, and Older-Sister sounds each of the basement steps like a dinner triangle as she rushes to come help too. My dad, so scared of the dark, turning off the kitchen light so as not to blind the owl suffering the broken wing, doing its best to retreat into the clatter of loose screwdrivers and many half-spent electrical tape rolls, something my uncles'd found stranded in some dead wood in the middle of the slough, its suffering golden eyes yellowing up the whole kitchen like a fresh-bulb floor lamp, its one wing broken but in some way I can't make sense of in this low light, some faulty geometry, its cry bad enough that I know it might never be mended, grounded forever and ever and its golden rings cast across the floor like a stunned Sonic, passing out from the shock of it all. The open toolbox lid looms, lifted, menacing like a backhoe bucket ready to bury nothing in particular at all.

eight months to a year

XAIVER MICHAEL CAMPBELL

I remember the day your brain ceded conscious control of your actions. To be precise, I remember the day it became obvious to me that your brain could no longer adapt to your surroundings. You could no longer speak or plan based on the decades' worth of stored information and amassed memories.

Synapses no longer travelling down neural pathways they once frequented.

The day before the day I noticed nothing would be the same was a normal, phenomenal day. Like most mornings, we woke with the sunrise, our bodies already intertwined. Everyday minutiae were all magical with you. That morning was the last one we would share. The day of the last sunrise, deep red lights crawled over the Narrows through the open window. The sounds of chatty birds and dogs celebrating being set free to do their business crept in to serenade us. The mattress on the floor was in the perfect spot to absorb the sun from morning till three p.m., when it passed beyond our view. Our position resulted in an eternal glare cast onto your laptop screen. We had countless mornings painted red. You wouldn't have it any other way.

It has been eight months since we watched a sunrise together. Eight months since you looked at me and touched me as a new morning burst forth. Eight months since we were us. The morning of our last sunrise you grabbed my dick. It always pulsed harder in your hands. Harder than it ever gets when I am with myself or any of the other nameless men I have used to pacify my own fragile mind.

In the eight months, you have grabbed my dick less than three times. Never at sunrise.

That morning, you came in me as we watched the sun ascend. As it claimed its spot in the sky, looking down over the city, I moaned your name. I thought it was like most mornings. My dick was still at home in your grasp. Now pulsing harder, leaking. The rest of the city would wake soon. Other morning lovers beginning, finishing, edging, searching.

"Towel's over there." Your foot knocked over the grey bong we had glued together last week. Our reflexes not quick enough to catch it. The room immediately reeked of burnt, stale resin.

"Shit. Shit. Shit." You always swore in multiples. Kisses the exact same way. Everyone who has met us knows this, including your cousins I met for the first time when we were lifted for the hora.

We were on a mattress, without sheets. On the floor. We had been there for three days. Most of those days we were naked. Only getting dressed to walk down the flights of vocal wooden stairs to the kitchen. We talked about getting a mini fridge, but that was eight months ago. The mattress is still on the floor. There are no sheets on it.

The bong residue remains.

We finessed the bong back together again and refilled it; we filled our lungs and fucked again. The scissors were dull, but I cut the ends of your unruly orange hair anyways.

"You don't need a video." You thought my repertoire extended into the realm of cosmetology. This trust made me feel able. Competent. That was not something I often thought about myself. When your brain broke, I drew on that trust a lot. More than I told anyone. More than I told you. Though I think you knew.

Two hours after we watched our last sunrise, we went outside. In seconds your cheeks turned that shade of pink that some would mistake for sunburn. Your eyes were always hazel, but in the sun, they turned a colour I'd never seen before. That crooked smile—which made all your features come alive—arrested me. The sight of you made me want to go back inside, back to our mattress. You felt like home. It has been eight months and I still wonder what would have happened if we had just gone back inside and fucked?

"What are you staring at?" You take much longer to get these words out now, the neural pathways being misaligned and all.

What am I staring at? The worse in for better or worse.

I said nothing.

The last time we watched the sunrise you walked me to work, which was our normal. It was the only way I would be early for the start of my shifts. I began decrying the woes of capitalism last year: instead of just eating the free egg salad, as we were permitted at work, I began adding two slices of bacon and a handful of jalapenos to each sandwich at lunch. My personal favourite was showing up to work a minute after the fifteen-minute grace period and never making eye contact with my overlords.

"Don't get yourself fired before you inherently and meaningfully change the system."

You warned that my silent protests amounted to petty theft and tardiness.

The raspberries shone like jewels through the towers of mile-a-minute that lined the sidewalk to the diner where I poured coffee. We pulled fruits off thorned branches without stopping. The berries were extra sweet even though it was hard to get enough sun behind the giant weeds. I tugged at your coat as we neared the middle of the weed-lined walkway.

"You're going to be late," you said.

I pursed my lips to lure you. Just one last kiss, I mouthed without sound.

"Oy, you're insatiable. You're going to be late." You usually knew better than me and often pushed me to do what would make me better. In every way. But if I'd known that was going to be the last time we'd watch the sunrise together, I would have insisted you fuck me in those bushes before my shift.

The last time we watched the sunrise together, I came home, and you were out for a walk. The last time we watched the sunrise together, you walked all night. The day after we watched our last sunrise, you slept through our morning rituals. You slept for what felt like forever but turned out to be four days. Once you pissed the bed, and I was glad for a sign of life. Sometimes, I wish you hadn't woken because when you did, it wasn't who I knew. There was no laughter. No words, your eyes barely open.

I would love the man who woke up, because I had no choice. You had the same face. The same musk that makes me foolish and uneasy. I searched for who I knew. For the oneness of us that I enjoyed the last time we watched the sunrise. I was too late. Too late for words, thoughts and prayers. A change had come, and we were what remained. These alien versions recognizable to others by allegedly identical visages. While you were fading in and out of sleep, we were withering farther and farther from this plane. Each other.

I remember the day after you woke up. It took you twenty-nine hours to speak. Your voice seized me in a familiar way, and I wished it were otherwise. Could this be a stranger and still the man I have loved my whole life?

"Who are you?" Your eyes, fearful, couldn't meet mine. You didn't reach for my dick. Your back, firmly planted against the wall. All I could do was think about the last time we watched the sunrise together. The last time we were one. It had been only days, but I wouldn't believe that if I had not lived it. Each day that your brain told you watching the sunrise with me was optional felt like ten thousand years.

I stayed home from work the day you woke up, the day you spoke. You hadn't eaten and now it had become crucial that something line the pit of your stomach. Water, if not food. Usually there would have been at least mouthfuls of my cum in your gut by now.

For the whole week she looked after you, we called her *the lady*.

"Now we know a lot." The lady in the plaid lab coat spoke to both of us, though she directed her attention to me. I don't know if there were hellos upon introduction. Security, nurse, intake, resident.

Then just this lady and us.

We all sat in a cramped office. There was a red string around her neck, I assumed her name was somewhere in the gold lanyard at the end of the string. Her hair pulled all the way up on her head and wrapped around itself so it couldn't be used against her, in situations like these.

"Now?" my voice trembled. I didn't know anything about what *now* meant. The only *now* I was forced to confront was the smell of the camphor balls coming off the lady.

"At this point in the twenty-first century. We know more about the brain. Though, admittedly, we still don't know everything." The lady spoke each word slowly and with her hands, a blank look in her eyes. Her pace gave me time to think of anything other than the smell of camphor balls, which erupted from her with each compulsive gesticulation. The office walls were all beige; the harsh, rectangular fluorescent bulb did nothing to help the room's or anyone's mood. You didn't seem to notice there were no windows, no natural light. There was a painting of the South Side Hills; the artist had reimaged the white Irving oil tanks orange. The painting itself was lovely, not abstract. I could tell what they were going for. Oddly enough, now, seeing the oil tanks orange, I decided I preferred them the stark white they are.

"His brain?" Now yanked back to the lady's voice, our conversation, the smell of the camphor balls. My grandma covered everything in camphor balls. You were wearing the red-and-cream knitted sweater Grandma once owned. Only eight months ago did we finally get rid of the camphor ball smell.

"The supplementary motor area (SMA), which is located at the centre of the medial frontal lobe network, was temporarily affected by an overload." The lady stared at me as she spoke. Still no life in her eyes. She reached over the stacks of papers on her narrow desk. There was a picture with a woman that looked like her and a man and three tiny children of various ages. She was smiling in the photo. Very white teeth. Teeth I had yet to see since we sat down. How does she break bad news to her family?

"His what?" I asked another question, since you seemed content with just listening.

"The SMA, being a premotor area on the frontal lobe's medial, is also a key structure that tells the brain how to behave . . ." About me, our life. She kept talking as if she were answering my questions. I looked back at the painting. The orange began to repulse me. My insides were welling up. The room lacked oxygen. You sat there, hands under your chin, eyes closed. Wearing my grandma's sweater. Why wasn't there a window? A plastic bag?

I breathed. Could they both taste the oxygen-less air? Was I really hearing all this?

"In your case, the result was a disruption of your ability to adapt and relate to your surroundings." The lady kept talking. She turned to you; her eyes narrowed, then the corners of them drooped a little bit. The lady was ready to feel.

"To me?" I focused on the orange oil tanks. No comfort to be found in you.

"And"—she gesticulated—"to you." This time I could read and feel her empathy.

When you woke up, your brain literally did not know me, how to interact with me. You didn't react to this or any of her words. We sat as she kept talking science and I thought of how all this new information was changing my brain. Our life. I wished there was silence.

"Afferent connections . . . The SMA is one of the universally connected areas of the brain . . . it is very rare . . . parietal lobes, which represent integrated knowledge of motor conditions . . . receives input from the hypothalamus, and from the basal ganglia." The lady continued, denying me the silence I wanted. Her gold lanyard was lined with other metals which shone under the fluorescent lights and made her name unreadable. She talked more; no one listened. We took pamphlets and she showed us our new home.

The day you spoke was the day we met the lady. Neither of us wanted to, nor did we have a choice. But there are systems in place that strip you of that choice if lines are considered crossed. Our part of town didn't afford lawns, let alone privacy. The houses dense like sardines and families piled up like Legos. Most of our neighbours were poorer than us, but we all lived the same and depended on all the same handouts the government could give. That day, everyone could hear you scream. Or they heard my own scream. The sirens and the doors banged wide open. Everyone saw you leave, not of your own accord.

Eight months later and we still don't know what caused the overload in your SMA. No one has been able to tell me how to reverse it either.

Since then, we have figured out a new normal. One that doesn't involve the sunrise, mind-blowing sex or mind-altering substances. There's just us and what we promised each other before family and friends.

I remember the day you didn't remember me. It has been eight months and I have thought about that day over five million times. What if the memory of me never came back? Would I really have been free? How could I be when I would still be strapped to you?

In the past eight months we have been to the hospital thirteen times. Three of those times you were there for over a week. We told everyone you were on a business trip, but you were mostly unemployed. Travelling for work was a stretch. The last time we went to the hospital was beyond the worst in the "for better and for worse" part of the promise.

The lady happened to be there every time. She often wore her plaid coat. I assume it was laundry day when she matched the rest of the staff. What was written on her name tag was still a mystery, even though she addressed us both by name with each committal.

"I am not Moshiach," I screamed in your ear as you held onto my shoulders, my ears pained at your suggestion. My faith before now has never appealed to you. Your breath stale from continuous sleep and refusing food and drink. I ran towards our front door, only you were somehow already blocking my way. It must have been when someone called the police. Control, lost.

"I feel the spirit of the Eternal Father in your veins," you kept saying, a conviction you felt to be more real than anything I have ever believed. There was a space between you and the door. I should have run, but what was once automatic, moments ago, was now unthinkable. To leave you, to get away. How could I?

I heard the sirens and the knock and the lights and the noise. And then the lady.

Then the lady again.

And again.

Each time, this place becomes more real. A known address in the GPS. Each time we walk through these doors, I think about the first time I realized something was wrong. Did I miss something, do something wrong?

"Hello again." The lady means well.

"It's no one's fault."

"It's him."

"Remember, there were prior signs. Signs that existed before you two even met. The brain always gives signs before it gets to this point. We just didn't know to look for them or even what they may have looked like." The lady discomforts with cold facts. Her arm around me does not achieve the intended effect, but maybe it does. It is uncertain, but I watch her gesticulate with her free hand. There is some strange comfort in that.

I can never remember my response because *for worse* has left me speechless. On these occasions, my SMA is traumatized.

In the eight months since our last sunrise, we have laughed only five times. A noise that used to echo through our walls and cause the neighbours to bang has vanished and left a hole inside me. We found that the blue ovals with the brown M take away your desire to burst out into characteristic fits of spontaneous laughter. One in the morning, one at lunch and another just before bed.

The orange ones make sure something else happens. By the time the lady gets to the details of the orange pills I am busy remembering the last sunrise. Everything since that red morning on the mattress has been new. What is made of each morning is up to us. Truly, it is up to you. I tend to follow your lead. In this way, our life is very much like how we have always been. Following your lead has turned me on since we first met. Remember how you could easily catapult my day? Our phones would die as we were wrapped up in each other, tucked away from everyone and everything. Your hand in mine.

One hundred and thirty-five days after the last sunrise, something happened. I opened our door. We held off on giving you back your keys, as advised by the lady. Our house lacked any trace of camphor balls. You walked directly to the couch and lay down. Your eyes confronted our furniture, the art on the walls, our plants, almost everything with a grimaced intimacy. Within moments you were asleep. I wrapped you in the knitted patchwork quilt that was draped over the couch. In the space between your legs, I planted my bottom and laid my feet by your ear. Your breathing was steady, a song I had been aching to hear.

"You're going to be late." I hadn't heard that timbre in your voice in months. It stirred hope inside me. It was the first time. The lady mentioned phases, breaks, glimmers. Your hand found mine.

"For what?" My schedule had changed months ago. Now I was the diner manager. My overlords made it clear tardiness and management do not go hand in hand. I had found other ways to decry the woes of capitalism. You didn't know this and your haste felt familiar. I was happy; it had been a while, I played along.

"Come on, let's go." We left our house. You took my hand. Fingers interlaced. It felt like home. My heart, in that moment, forgot everything. We had sun, it was cold, but there was no precipitation. And it was you. There in the same eyes. It was the first time since our last sunrise, only now you could see through your eyes. You could see me. That look. Crooked smirk. No good. Home.

"Wanna fuck in the bushes?" You pulled me closer, and we looked over at the decimated fruit trees and shrubs. The ground had frozen while you were away. "The bathroom at the diner?" A single raised eyebrow, your hands shoved down my pants.

"Are you sure?" My body welcomed your touch. "Did you take your pill?" I managed foolish words between the sensation of your lips on my neck.

The pink in your cheeks surfaced. Your hands found your own pockets. Moment over. Old life really gone. There are no more bongs to tip over because the purple pills require zero competition from other narcotics for them to work. The lady was insistent, she snapped me out of my trance so I could hear all about the purple pill. Fucking up the purple pill could lead to the white pills and she was adamant we never wanted the white. Now we have three different broken teapots by the floor of the bed. All an arm's length from the electric kettle we picked up from someone's trash on a drive through Mount Pearl.

You had an episode in the restaurant on our anniversary. The blue pill failed to perform. Broken glass on hardwood floors. Customers rushing out. Sirens. More sirens.

"Hello again." Did the lady take pleasure in seeing us? Was she just paid to be polite?

"I am not Moshiach," I begged, hoping this was my own lapse and not what I knew it was.

"Maybe not how you think He is. I can see Him. Let me show you." You stepped towards me; I inched away.

That night I left you there with her. I released the devil in me. With another.

"You're human," you reminded me the next morning when I returned, since nothing remained hidden between us.

"Kind man. I don't deserve ..."

You brushed your lips against mine before I could finish.

The lady pulled strings for us that night. It was my first night with you in your home away from home.

"You're almost regulars." There was not even a hint of that camphor ball smell coming off the lady when she put her hand on my shoulder and squeezed.

We stayed there. It was the longest time we had lain together since the last sunrise.

One morning we roused ourselves in that tiny hospital bed before any light had graced the sky. It had been almost a year since we watched the sunrise. In minutes, the sterile white room was painted red and gold. The colours blended and faded in and out in dynamic shapes.

"Hello." You laughed. I swept a tuft of orange ringlets from your eyes; I was grounded.

Your laughter incapacitated me. Eventually I plugged your mouth to block the sound. The feel of your pout jump-started me. You moved my hand and pressed your soft lips on mine. I could breathe again.

The lady walked by, and we were both immobile. Soon, I started laughing and you joined in. The next sound I made was the one that often followed you grabbing my dick. It had been a while, but we still fit. There were no mountains to look at. My eyes focused on the scribbles, lore and warnings the previous occupants left behind. I prayed that M.C + E.B = 4EVA to this day, since long-lasting love in these situations can end prematurely. We moved as one on that bed as if no time had passed. Hope, yellows, joy, and white light all flooded into that blood-stained room. I could have stayed there forever, and sometimes I wonder if I am still there. Stuck in the dream of the last time we watched the sunrise.

The next day, the orange pill was the culprit.

We realized we didn't know what was what. We'd trusted in our love. We knew for better or for worse, in sickness and in health, and till death do us part.

"Hello again," the lady will say.

"Hello Gloria," I will answer.

the flat freshie blue-star test

HEIDI WICKS

The nylon tent is smeared and streaked with splashes of beer, dabs of red-yellow ketchup-mustard, droplets of malt vinegar and french-fry grease and slippery fingerprints.

Stark naked inside its flimsy, floppy structure, Jane steps into a dry pair of denim cut-offs and pulls on a fresh tank. Outside, she can hear the cracking open of beer cans, the sucking open of chip bags and the rustling of other flimsy, floppy structures nearby.

B'y. Jim Hibbs spits on the ground outside the tent. The sound makes Jane retch. *I never t'ought we'd come out alive.*

The drive from St. John's to Grand Falls had been treacherous. Blowing down the Trans-Canada, a '92 silver Chrysler jammed with belligerent teens. Jane's head was stuck out the passenger window, strands of hair batting against each other, whipping and whapping the window behind her.

I'm like a biirrrd! Jane belted the Nelly Furtado song into the gusts. Nelly would be live, on stage, in Grand Falls, in hours. When Jane opened her eyes and saw the Holsum buns truck boinging too close in front of them, Adam yapping away at Jim through the rear-view mirror, his eyes only half on the road, Jane's heart punched her in the throat and she shrieked, ADAM! And Adam jumped and swerved quickly, the full carload of them squealing in terror.

Mommy! Mommy! Jim Hibbs didn't even know he was saying it.

Hail Mary Full of Graaaaaace, Nicole's long, hot-pink nails dug into Jim's arm until crescent-shaped blood marks formed in his flesh.

The car bumped over the gravel, the undercarriage skidding against rocks until the poor Chrysler thumped into a *poof I give up* breath on the shoulder of the road.

The four of them, agog, frozen in time, wondering if they were dead or alive, on the shoulder of the Trans-Canada. They stayed there, dumbfounded, in silence, ambivalent about the rush of cars on the road, too utterly shitbaked to even draw a breath, until the hush was broken by the whisper of branches over yonder. A moose stood, chewing slowly, glaring at the carful of stupidity. The Holsum truck was far down the road, its urge to gobble up the Chrysler now passed, trapped in a Trans-Canada time capsule, along with thousands of other perilous brushes with death.

They cracked their doors open and stepped outside the car.

Jesus Christ, b'ys, sorry about that. Adam's skinny legs trembled as he tried not to piddle in his Fruit-of-the-Looms. That was pretty fucked, wasn't it?

Yes, Adam, Jim's eyes were wide like fried eggs. That was just a bit fucked, Adam.

Y'all right, Jim? Adam walked like he just stepped off a pony.
Yes, buddy. Legs got pins n' needles, das all. You all right?
Yes, my buddy, I'm all right.

Yeah, I'm all good too, Adam, by the way! Jane thought, as she walked around the back of the car to hug Nicole and shoot Adam the stink eye before stalking towards the woods to squat. She'd been holding her pee since Clarenville.

This is the most satisfying pee of my entire life. She said it to no one except the sky. The contents of her bladder splashed onto the dirt and sprayed the branches and she felt a warm firework on her leg and shot her butt backwards and held her underwear up, but it was too late. She shook it off and shrugged it off and hauled up her pants.

Somethin' smells like pee, Adam said, once they started driving again.

They pulled over for gas before they started the last leg of the drive.

Ya got gas? The cashier's bark shot out loud and gravelly from underneath her bouffant yellow-tinged hair and through her thin lips. *DOT*, read her nametag. All capital letters with a period at the end. Don't-fuck-with-me-Dot.

Oh, no. Jane pushed the Vachon cake across the counter towards Dot. Just this.

Dot jabbed her long pink nail at the cash register. Clickety-clack-clicked at the keys. Chewed her gum like a coked-up cow eating grass. Focused. On a mission. A let's-get-this-over-with-so-I-can-finish-my-Jesus-conversation-please kind of energy.

Seventy-five cents. Dot stopped chewing and glared at Jane. Spat the over-chewed gum into the garbage can and it pinged off the side like a bullet, it was so hard. Sneered out the window at Adam screwing on the top to the gas tank. Looked back at Jane. Rolled her eyes at Adam.

Jane slid a loonie towards Dot and Dot snatched it away. Dot wouldn't make eye contact with Jane again. Their transaction in this world was complete.

Jane passed the snack-size cake, filled with wholesome chemicals, to Adam and he snatched it away like Dot had snatched her money.

No Joe Lou-eeze? Adam scowled.

No Joe Louis. *Say thank you, say thank you.* Whenever he was mean she withered a little, which made her mad.

He flipped the ignition.

Buckled up? Adam whipped his neck towards Jane, with his perfect teeth and his perfect blue eyes, beaming with pride over his own sense of responsibility and the benevolent message of care he'd just delivered to his friends. He planted one on her cheek and she felt her insides glow toasty warm. The classic, addictive Adam upswing. Up and down, up and down. She never did like rollercoasters, but she couldn't resist. Hey. Thanks for the cake, sweet buns. And there it was. The gut dive she felt when being taken advantage of, erased by affection. The salvation. The thing that keeps her there.

The Chrysler bounced in sober silence, none of them saying much until they pulled into Redcliff. The car and the bodies within collectively exhaled when Adam turned the engine off.

As soon as they pulled into the campsite, Adam cracked a beer and handed it to her as she crouched to pull the tent poles from the bag. *Aw, he gave me my beer first*—and she hated herself for thinking it. They assembled the tent together, without words.

I'll be out there somewhere, all right? Adam grabbed himself another beer once they were done and turned towards the conglomerate of skeets and snobs and bay people and townies in their teens and twenties and thirties and forties and god-knows-how-much-older. One big punchbowl of shitmix, down below, dancing, drunk, on drugs, all night long. Club Relentless.

Jane is relieved to be alone in the tent. Peeling off her pissy shorts, she debates finding a campground water source to clean herself off a bit but figures "what odds?" and lies on her back in her underwear. The afternoon band is getting on the go—she hears them warming up on stage. Honeymoon Suite. Again.

Staring at the translucent blue material of the tent ceiling, she imagines the scene on the field: bare chests with wiry white and brown hairs sprouting from the loose hot-dog-red skin. Pores that smell like Labbatt's. Breath that smells like smokes. The legs of their camping chairs denting the grass, forming ravines of entitlement. First ones on the field, me buddy. They're here for the Honeymoon Suite. Give 'em the Chilliwack. April Wine 'em. Nelly Fur-what-oh? Can't be bothered.

From the oceanic blue ecosphere of the tent, Jane absorbs her surroundings. The campsite is electric with other concertgoers and partiers. A wackload of high school kids and twenty-somethings (who were considered old).

She recently read *The Electric Acid Kool-Aid Test* by Tom Wolfe. There's a scene where the Beatles drive on a psychedelic school bus with the Merry Pranksters to a music festival in California. The whole crowd just throbs there together, like one giant organism. A year later, *Magical Mystery Tour* is released. They're all on their way to Further—their final destination, which can only be reached through the expansion of one's perception of reality.

Tucked in the safety of her amniotic tent sac, she imagines the crowd outside, surrounding her, below her, all of the skeets and the scullies and the snobs and the bay people and the townies and the teens and twenty- and thirty- and forty-fifty-sixty-year-olds and they're all buzzing and humming in unison on some vibration, waiting for her to join the one giant organism.

Except instead of California and LSD and the Beatles and Ken Casey and the Merry Pranksters on a psychedelic school bus, it's Newfoundland and skunk weed and Chilliwack and a shit-hauled silver Chrysler.

But who knows? Nelly Furtado might be one stop closer to Further.

The smell of propane and roasting wieners resurrects Jane, suddenly ravenous, from her solitude. Brings her out to the light. She emerges to satiate a primal need for sustenance. A charred wiener, globby with BBQ sauce, drenched in ketchup and mustard and relish, and she devours it, for it's the only thing available to fill the void in her gut. When she steps from the tent, the early evening sun is still hot on her face. She splashes back the rest of her beer.

Hey, neighbour. The voice startles Jane. A woman, thirty-something, Jane guesses, is pitching a tent about twenty feet from theirs. Her accent isn't local. Her eyes are sleepy and peaceful and sparkly. Her hair is teased into bleached-blond dreads and she's wearing denim shorts and a flowery kimono. A tiny hoop through her left nostril. Bangles gangle around her wrist. She smells like patchouli and sun-baked skin. The sun is directly behind her and it looks like she has a halo.

I'm Marcia. She lifts her chin briefly and her pupils bore soulfully into Jane's. *Are her eyes purple?* Her metallic eyeshadow gives them an ethereal glimmer.

Here with some mates, ay?

Yeah, my boyfriend and our friends. A ton of people from our school and other high schools are here.

Jane squints at Marcia.

Right. Well, I'll let yeh git to 'em.

What school do you go to?

Oh—Marcia appears bemused. I'm not in high school, mate.

I'm here with my partner. We're travelling this summer and figured we'd stop by. See what all the noise is about.

It's not often that Jane feels like she has to impress anyone. Marcia sends her a warm, chilled-out, droopy-eyed smile and flashes Jane the peace symbol. Jane flips back a peace sign, imagining they are passing sunbeams back and forth.

Cool. Well, I better go find my boyfriend, I guess.

Y'don't seem too eager! Marcia laughs.

Well if I'm being honest—Jane takes a step closer—it's not like it used to be. But whatever.

Marcia winks at Jane. Yeah. Whatever is right.

Hey, maybe we can have a beer or something later.

Sure thing. Marcia is amused.

As Jane walks away, another woman steps out of Marcia's tent and wraps her arms around Marcia's midsection and they are cheek-to-cheek, swaying to and fro, and the sight sends a ripple of something through Jane's own middle.

Jane!—Adam hollers from part way down the hill—Let's GO, babe! She walks towards him, making sure to hesitate a little. Nicole is close by, so they lace fingers and move ahead of the boys, leading them into the crowd. The last of the bare-chested Honeymoon Suite men fold their lawn chairs and tuck them under their arms and waddle towards the sidelines. The field's energy bubbles like beer carbonation, ready to explode.

Moving through the clammy bodies, the sea of bobble heads, suddenly, inches from Jane's face is the face of her mother's friend Sheila. Since the day Jane was brought home from the hospital, there was their neighbour Sheila, with a tray of Flakies and a tin of Pepsi. Do you want a Flakie, girls? It was her offering at any social gathering. The last person Jane expected to see in the middle of Salmon Fest. She grasps Jane's arm.

Jane! Christ on a cross, how are ya, me duck? Bein' a good girl out here, are ya?—Sheila cackles and she scans Jane. My gawd girl, you're gawn some skinny!

Jane smooths her hands over her behind and remembers the hot dog she just scarfed back.

Oh, I don't know—Jane tucks one hand into the pocket of her shorts, making sure she can still feel her hip bone as she flashes to the *Seventeen* magazine she flipped through on the car ride here. All of the expectations of having a boyfriend and staying skinny, like it's the whole world. She thinks back to the cupboard of Flakies at Sheila's. The sickly chemical smell as Sheila peeled off the wrapper and placed the pastry on a plate in front of Jane, waiting for her to eat it and enjoy it every bit as much as Sheila did every evening while she watched *The Price Is Right*. Jane could see her at it, licking every last bit of cream out of the middle, through her living room sheers while Jane was outside shovelling the driveway.

Adam has taken Jane's other hand and she lets him tug her along, weave her quickly through the crowd.

Bye, Sheila! Jane calls behind her, and Sheila disappears from sight, folding in among her demographic, being swallowed by the youth. Jane does feel like she's in the process of losing weight.

Cigarette smoke and marijuana smoke and BBQ smoke and smoked dry ice machines cloud the atmosphere into a dance-club vibe. Making their way towards the stage is like ascending into the heavenliest section of hell. The light is dripping from the sky, melting from orange to purply blue. Dusk spreads a dark veil over the day.

Babe. Let's go! Adam is excited. He twists his fingers into hers and strokes the front of her index finger as they walk and she shivers. She hates it that he can create that feeling inside her.

After a while, Nicole's fingers slip from Jane's grasp so it's just her and Adam now, and they're getting so close to the stage, so close to where Nelly Furtado will be.

Brenda O'Neil is in the crowd. In grade nine, Brenda O'Neil inexplicably turned around in her desk in the middle of science class and stabbed Jane in the hand with a sharp pencil. If *what the fuck?* had been in Jane's vernacular at the time, she would have shouted it at Brenda and attacked her right back. Instead, she teared up, painfully, hormonally, shy and unsure of herself, wondering why on earth someone would do that, except to See Jane Cry.

The drum thumps get louder and harder in her chest, the hot smells of hundreds, probably thousands of people—unwashed hair, strawberry-scented Body Shop body spray, fruity lip balm, beer yeast, smoke, sweat—the organism throbs.

Hellooo, Grand Falls! Nelly Furtado is there, herself like a bird—a hummingbird. Dainty and gutsy and electric, exploding with quick sparks. She bops her fist into the air and skips and bounces across the stage, her chirpy voice turning each audience member into a fizzy drink. A pixie sprinkling dust. Her star presence is enigmatic in Newfoundland.

Are we gonna have some FUN tonight?

The crowd whoops and squeals and Jane cranes her neck. They are only about fifty feet from the stage now, and she wants to be on Adam's shoulders, right up front, swaying collectively with that wretched audience, every last one of them, absorbing that electric Kool-Aid flat Freshie Blue-Star energy pulsing within that great stinking orb that is the Salmon Festival.

Adam has grabbed her hips and is grunting, squirming, trying to hoist her up on his shoulders. She jumps to try to help him gain some momentum, and his weight and hers wobble on his skinny legs, but he holds it together and by the Jesus, he does it! He gets her up on his shoulders. Jane's gaze flits around the crowd like a hummingbird seeking nectar. It's a blurred wash of colours and movement, like a Monet painting, or like a drug-induced scene in *Fear and Loathing in Las Vegas*, no identifiable faces, except . . . is that . . .

Marcia. She's right next to the stage, not twenty feet away from Jane and Adam. She catches Jane's eye and shoots her the same cinnamon-toast-smile, warm and sweet and buttery and nourishing, and she flashes the peace sign again. *Our special thing.*

The red and orange stage lights are hot on Jane's face. The giant black speakers make her ears throb so loud that she feels her lymph nodes reverberate, and she feels the pulse travel down into her throat and chest and guts. She closes her eyes and lets the thump of the amplifiers shake her entire body and brain and she has succumbed to the moment. It is only her in that crowd, underneath that light, just as it was only her earlier, in the blue light of the tent.

Sweat springs to her forehead and drips down into her eyes, down the bridge of her nose. When she lifts a hand to wipe it away, she loses her balance. Adam starts to sway, too many beers, and she grips onto him for dear life, clenches her thighs around his neck.

Jesus, Jane, yer chokin' me! he barks.

She wills him to regain his balance. *Don't fail me.* The bodies squeezed tight around him stabilize him and she breathes a millisecond-long sigh of relief until time slows down and speeds up and then slows down, the pulses turn to throbs in her ears and throat, sounds are muted and warbly, just like on the highway with the Holsum truck, and then, BOOM. She is on the ground and sound is silenced. Above her, dozens of heads and arms and bodies bump together until the purply dusk above is eaten by a horde of limbs and heads. Blackness.

Eyes blink open, slow, sloth speed. Head feels like it's been blasted with a concrete floor-grinder. Above her, blurred paint strokes of muted colours. Her skin tingles. She shivers.

She senses lilac. Marcia.

Hey there . . . you're okay. Marcia's accent soothes Jane's pounding head. Her hand cups Jane's. I saw you go down. It must've been so scary, love.

Jane is back in her own tent. She has vague memories of Marcia helping her back there from the first-aid tent.

Here. Have some Freshie. Marcia puts a cup to Jane's lips. The drink is tangy and sweet.

Where's Adam?

He's out on the field, love.

Pfft. Jane is surprised to feel absolutely nothing besides possibly relief. She'd much rather be here with Marcia, anyway.

How old are you? Jane surprises herself by asking the question.

Marcia laughs. I'm twenty-seven.

Twenty-seven's a great age. Jimi Hendrix, Janis Joplin, Jim Morrison, Kurt Cobain—they all died at twenty-seven.

Well jeez, I hope I don't *die* at twenty-seven. But I must admit I'm surprised you know about all those legends. A bit ageist of me, I know it, I'm not proud of it, I'm sorry. How old are you?

I'm eighteen.

Ah. Finishing high school?

Yup.

So . . . what's next?

The flap of Jane's tent opens and the woman whose arms were wrapped around Marcia's waist earlier is there holding a pitcher of Freshie. Refill?

Ah. Jane, this is my partner, Belinda.

Hey Belinda.

Jane—Marcia holds out her hand—would you like to walk

back out there together?

The three of them link arms, Jane in the middle.

So—Marcia asks again—what's next? What's after high school?

The stars are bright, despite the stage light.

Marcia, do you ever feel like there's tar in your lungs, or on your chest?

I think I know what you mean. Just, heavy. Stuck. Is this about Adam?

I think so. Partly, anyway. I just feel like I want . . . more. And not more *from* him. More *besides* him.

When a relationship is starting to end, I always think of a tree being chopped down, and that first chop. You always remember what the first chop is. You know it's never gonna be the same after the first chop.

Jane knows what the first chop was: During the thirty-hour famine school sleepover, about six months ago. It was so late that it was almost light again. Jane and Adam stood in the porch of the school, in their pyjamas, their eyes sleepy. The morning sun was just starting to push the night sky up and away—like a grocer pushing open the garage door to his shop to begin the day. Jane confided that she wanted to go tree planting in BC, and Adam spat his drink out and laughed and laughed and told her she was a hippie.

Even though she's no longer right next to the stage, Jane still feels just as connected with the pulse and the heartbeat of the crowd. The lights and sounds buzz in her ears and settle onto her chest and nestle into her being.

When Adam and Jim and Nicole stumble back to the tent that night, Jane is sitting around the fire with Marcia and Belinda.

Bayyyybeeee, I was lookin' fer ya, Adam lays a wet slobbery

kiss on her mouth and she scrunches her nose and yanks her face away from his. Adam doesn't notice.

Nicole cuddles in next to her, droopy-eyed. Girlfriend, I missed you! How could you leave me with these two arseholes?

Adam and Jim have joined in with a horde of high school kids smoking a draw nearby and Nicole sleeps next to Jane in the tent.

Janey. Nicole's head is on Jane's shoulder the next morning as they sip a Diet Pepsi before packing up. Do you want to get back in the car with the guys tomorrow? That accident . . . she drifts off for a minute . . . that freaked me out.

Yeah. Jane stares at the campers surrounding her, wearily packing up their gear and slopping back Gatorade. I'd rather just . . . not.

Marcia and Belinda have space in their car, ya know, Nick. We could just not go with the guys. I bet they'd give us a lift.

Yeah, fuck it, shrugs Nicole. Let's just not!

Adam's not a bad guy, thinks Jane. He can be sweet, spontaneous, silly, affectionate and he used to bring out her sparkle. He lives in the moment. He loves his friends. He loves to party. It's why he's so lovable. But Jane is beyond the present. Jane is dreaming of the future. Of what's next. *Are ya comin' with me, buddy?* she silently asks Adam, every time she looks at him. She knows the answer.

Tree planting lies ahead. California. Who knows, really.

Who needs a bumpy ride back home when you could take the smooth, freshly paved road to Further?

effie

OLIVIA ROBINSON

Effie and I fell into friendship at the gas station down the road from the high school. It was one of those early September days that still held the heat of summer, and it was easy to forget about school and slip back into the timelessness of August. Every lunch hour, a group of us traipsed down the gravel shoulder of the highway for coffee. We shoved each other into the ditch and people in passing cars laid on their horns as we darted into the road and leapt onto each other's backs.

We were reading *Twelfth Night* in English class, which was where I first met Effie. I loved listening to her read aloud because her voice sounded full, like she was coming down with a cold or had just swallowed a glug of chocolate milk. She was an exchange student from Denmark and had the hint of a lisp she had learned to suppress. I was desperate to get to know her so I could listen to her talk all the time.

At the gas station, I drowned my lukewarm coffee with milk and sugar, pretending to like the taste because the novelty of buying it made me feel grown-up. Effie took her coffee black. She bought a flaky strawberry pastry and went outside, where she leaned against the wall next to the air pump. I went and stood beside her and without a word she ripped open the plastic bag, tore the pastry in half, and gave me the bigger piece. Strawberry jam oozed onto her fingers and she licked it off.

A man in beige coveralls was crouched down filling the tires of his Ford, and I could feel him watching us. I had started to learn that being female was the only requirement for that type of man, the type who stared too long in a way that made me feel exposed, like I was being evaluated for something I wasn't even sure I wanted.

When Effie noticed the man staring, she straightened her posture.

"Hey you! Creepy man! Didn't your mother teach you not to stare?"

Effie crumpled up the plastic wrapper and threw it in his direction. It fluttered to the ground a few feet away and the man smirked. I saw the corner of Effie's mouth twitch in anger and I put my arm on hers but she stepped forward anyway and poured the rest of her coffee over the hood of his truck.

The man stood and glared at us, his confidence fading fast into anger. In the span of a few seconds, we had become entirely different girls.

"You little sluts," he said through gritted teeth as he climbed into his truck. The tires squealed as he reversed and tore out of the parking lot.

Effie and I shared the rest of my coffee on the way back to school. We walked slowly, lagging behind the rest of the group. Effie was laughing and trying to recreate the man's facial expressions. I laughed too, but my heart was pounding.

After school, the bus dropped us off in the mall parking lot.

We sat in the food court eating soft pretzels and drinking blue slushies, the food colouring turning our tongues and lips blue. We tried on clothes and hats and Effie took pictures of us with a disposable camera. She modelled a bright orange stocking cap and a hat that looked like a raccoon. We left the mall with our arms linked and stood under a streetlight in the parking lot to wait for my grandmother to pick us up. The afternoon had faded into the blue of evening and as we stood there, the light turned on, plunging us into a golden spotlight. I turned my head to look at Effie and she smiled and leaned forward to kiss me. Her blue lips tasted like the sugary slushie and I wondered if mine did too. We were surrounded by a haze of naivety so thick it shimmered, existing in that strange fog between childhood and adulthood where everything was hilarious and beautiful and it was impossible to define the difference between friendship and love.

The school year passed in a blur of soccer practice, trips to the gas station, and evenings spent studying and watching movies in Effie's bedroom. It was a windowless space in the basement of her host family's home, a messy but sparsely furnished room with a bed and pressboard dresser. There were clothes strewn everywhere and a suitcase with a broken wheel sat rejected in the corner. The room smelled like Effie, a mixture of sweaty soccer socks and the almond cream she rubbed on her elbows. We didn't talk about her impending return to Denmark but as the days grew warmer I thought about it constantly.

We studied for final exams, textbooks propped open against pillows, eating stale candy Effie had brought from home until our teeth ached. Effie's parents wanted her to be a doctor, so she took school very seriously and studied with enviable intensity, chewing the end of her pencil. By comparison I was a distracted, lazy student. I couldn't study without background noise, so we watched movies, alternating between two of our favourites, *Bend It Like Beckham* and *10 Things I Hate about You*.

But Effie didn't leave me as soon as I feared she would. Before our final English exam, she came over to the house where I lived with my grandmother. We studied in the screened-in sun porch, a room filled with plants and floral print furniture and the earthy smell of early spring sunshine. My grandmother, who looked like Lily Tomlin and wore bedazzled jeans, left an entire package of Oreos on the counter for us and disappeared. While we studied, I tried to memorize everything about Effie, how she ate like she was ravenous, the practised motion of sweeping her bangs out of her eyes. She wore a watch with a narrow leather strap on her left wrist. I was jealous of her, how easily she seemed to exist and know who she was. Now I wish I had paid more attention to the things we talked about, too, but memory is unfair and fleeting. Before bed, we brushed our teeth at the same time, making faces at each other in the mirror, our mouths frothy with gritty baking soda toothpaste.

We slept in my double bed but I couldn't fall asleep because I had forgotten to close the curtains. A rectangle of light from the street slanted in through the window, illuminating the end of the bed and our legs under the blankets. I was suddenly very conscious of being in my body, the feeling of skin tingling over bone all the way from my toes to my forehead. Effie nudged my calf with her foot and asked me if I was awake. I nodded and rolled over on my side to face her.

"My mom wants me to stay a little longer," Effie said. "She's leaving my dad and thinks it will be easier if I stay until she gets settled in her new apartment."

"I'm sorry," I said, but my heart was pounding with the gift of more time. "You can come with me and my gran to the cottage.

She's picking me up tomorrow after our exam."

Effie nodded in the shadows, her hair rustling against the pillow. "I'd like that."

She reached for my hand under the covers and we fell asleep.

In late June, the water was cold but we swam until the skin on our fingers and toes turned wrinkly. Effie liked to dive, slipping under the water almost soundlessly. She wore a blue one-piece bathing suit with a black T-shirt on over top. In the water she looked sleek and streamlined, like a cormorant. She swam out far, disappearing into the sunshine sparkling on the water and I waved at her with both arms until she swam back to me. She climbed out of the lake onto the dock and drops of water clung to her eyelashes like tiny pieces of confetti until she blinked them away.

We put temporary tattoos on the backs of our necks. Effie held up her hair while I applied a gold star below her right ear. I drew the Canadian flag on her ankle in black pen so it looked like a real tattoo. Effie applied a tiny silver moon at the nape of my neck as well, the cool cotton cloth sending goosebumps down my spine. The tattoos didn't last long because we spent so much time in the water. After a couple of days they became sticky blobs on our skin.

An old motorboat bobbed alongside the dock like a lost duck. Effie and I cleaned out the dead leaves, wiped off the vinyl seats, and spent every evening sitting in the boat reading. Our wet hair dripped small puddles on the seats and our fingers made the pages of our novels damp and crinkled. We stayed in the boat until it was too dark to see and held hands on the walk from the dock to the cottage, tiptoeing in our bare feet, shrieking in mock fear as bats swooped overhead through the pine trees.

There were two bedrooms in the cottage, a mezzanine level above the kitchen where my grandmother slept and a tiny room with bunk beds. The room smelled like damp wood and the rubber raincoats hanging on pegs on the wall. Effie put her stuff on the top bunk and messed up the sheets so it would look like she had slept there before folding herself into the bottom bunk with me. Her hair fanned out on the pillow smelled like the lake and her apricot shampoo, and we listened to the unearthly call of the loon through the open window.

My grandmother made us hot chocolate in the mornings when we stumbled into the golden kitchen with our messy hair and voices sandy with sleep. We cradled the mugs and sat on tall stools by the island, the smooth countertop cool under my elbows. My grandmother disappeared outside to drink her coffee on the porch in her pink fuzzy bathrobe. I watched Effie rub the sleep from her eyes. She took a sip of hot chocolate, her lips pursed on the edge of the mug, her round face still flushed.

I wanted time to stop so I could figure out how to say everything I wanted to say. I hated myself for being so shy and unsure. We spent the heat of the afternoons in the hammock strung in the shade between two pine trees, our heads at opposite ends, bare legs stuck together in the middle. I could feel the stubble on Effie's legs, the pale hairs visible against her tanned skin. We read or talked and sometimes drifted in and out of sleep, our eyes heavy from so much fresh air. We moved to the boat in the evenings when the air cooled, pulling on sweaters. I wore Effie's hoodie with her name on the sleeve and the logo of her soccer team in Denmark on the back and she wore my plain lilac hoodie. Both sweaters were baggy and reached halfway down our thighs and made me feel like I could disappear within the fabric. I wanted to tell Effie I didn't want her to leave and how terrified I was to go back to school. I didn't want to be forced to figure out who I was all over again without her.

"Let's promise to keep in touch, okay?" I said one night in the boat.

Effie had her legs pulled up to her chest and a book propped open on her knees.

"Of course," she said, smiling at me. "I have a telephone."

I laughed and she did too, nudging my leg with her knee before she returned her attention to her book. I wondered what would happen if she didn't have to go back to Denmark, if we could stay at the cottage forever in a perpetual August, who we would become if we had more time.

On the drive into town the next morning, we fell asleep in the back seat of my grandmother's car, still wearing each other's sweaters. We were dropping Effie off at the mall so she could buy a new suitcase. Her host family was meeting her there and they were leaving for the airport shortly after. My grandmother waited in the car while I walked in with Effie, our arms linked. We went to the food court and got blue slushies and drank them slowly.

We stopped by the gumball machines and I watched tears rise in Effie's eyes even though she was smiling. I could tell she was scared too, of what everything meant and the unknown life she was returning to. I stepped forward and we held each other for a long time. She still smelled like the lake and sunscreen. I tried not to think about how the next day she would be somewhere entirely different and the smell of the lake would fade from her hair. There was no discussion about returning the sweaters to their rightful owners.

I couldn't watch her leave. We both turned away and I broke into a run, my flip-flops slapping against the tile floor. I threw myself out the doors, back into the late August heat.

The last time we spoke on the phone Effie's voice was quiet and hollow, travelling along the transatlantic cable like a sound-wave fish. It was the summer before we started university and we wished each other good luck and promised to stay in touch. Our letters, which we used to write weekly and often ran for five or six pages, became shorter and farther apart until eventually they stopped altogether. Our monthly phone calls became less frequent until they also came to an end. As often happens with childhood friends, we faded apart, but I can't remember now who stopped replying first.

I have a picture of us framed on my desk at the library where I work; we're in the hammock at my grandmother's cottage, asleep, wearing each other's sweaters. Effie's face is turned toward the camera while mine is turned away. My co-workers asked who the girls were; a few assumed they were my daughters and I didn't correct them. I searched for Effie online recently and found her profile, my cursor hovering over the "add friend" button. In her profile picture, she was wearing a white lab coat and a wide smile. She had achieved what she set out to do and I wondered what would happen if I reached out again. But maybe there are certain people you can love only for a moment before they have to leave you.

Sometimes, when I was in a large crowd, I had the strange sensation that I was falling. This feeling had intensified in the ten years since I graduated from university and occurred at random times. For a few moments there was nothing beneath me, and then the feeling of hitting the ground again, a shock akin to touching an electric fence. A parcel had arrived for me at the library where I worked; it was sitting on my desk when I got in for the day. I sat in my chair and stared at the brown paper and the airmail sticker. My name and the address of the library were written in a careful cursive I knew as well as my own handwriting.

When I felt the chair underneath me again, I pulled the parcel toward me. It was a large, soft bubble envelope and I felt a twinge of excitement, wondering what Effie had sent, if this meant we could be in touch again. I sliced the parcel open with scissors and felt a familiar fabric in my hands.

The hoodie, which had been large on me when I was fifteen, would fit perfectly now. I resisted the desire to hold the sweater to my face because I knew there was no chance it still smelled like her. It had probably spent many years in a drawer or a closet or a cardboard box. I shook the envelope, searching for a note. The sweater had travelled across the sea in the belly of an airplane, all alone. Effie's sweater, the one from the soccer team with her name on the sleeve, was still folded in my bottom drawer. I hadn't worn it in years but I liked knowing it was there, a little piece of her I got to keep.

The picture of us in the hammock had been retired to my desk drawer, but I reached for it now to remind myself what we had looked like. I propped the photo against the sweater and looked at Effie's round face, framed by the lilac hood, her eyes closed. The person who was supposed to be me, with her light brown hair, had one arm draped over Effie's waist, and I wondered what had happened to that girl. I didn't recognize her at all.

lord gushue's reign of terror

WILLIAM PING

On the day that Brad Gushue competes for gold, we don't even have classes. They put the entire student body and faculty of Macpherson Elementary in the gym, with the TV at the front of the room, and the whole school watches as Gushue throws cement pucks across a man-made slab of ice in a faraway land. His sidekicks, Mark and Jamie, sweep the ice in front of the puck with Swiffer picker uppers, while Gushue and a coterie of other men yell "Hurry, hurry hard." They call this "curling," but I've never heard of it before.

Curling? More like boring.

I remain seated on the floor of the gym as the other kids and teachers jump to their feet with excitement. I have a well-worn *Magic Tree House* book, *Winter of the Ice Wizard*, to keep me occupied while these fools lose their minds over a little square with a frosty rectangle and a bunch of ant people playing

Raisinet shuffleboard with the occasional mulleted close-up.

"He's really going to do this," someone says.

"Do what?" I say without looking up from my earmarked pages.

"Win the gold!"

"Pffft, I got a bronze back home," I say, thinking fondly of the medal I had won in soccer two years earlier when I was eight years old. Sure, my bronze was more of a participation medal than any sort of recognition for actual sportsmanship on my part. If the ball came near me, I ran away. Rival teams loved it when I was goalie.

Sports were never my thing and if I can get a medal, then anybody can. It takes more than a disc of precious metal to impress me.

When Gushue throws his last puck and secures the gold, the entire gymnasium erupts into cheers. Big whoop. Can we get back to biology class now? Gushue's inside the crackly TV halfway across the gym and he's crying while talking on a flip phone. Everyone always told me boys weren't supposed to cry.

"Oh my Jesus, he's calling his mom!" Mrs. St. Croix is ecstatic. "This is Newfoundland history!"

Actually, the first transatlantic call was in 1901 and *that* was Newfoundland history, and we'd know that if we actually had class today instead of watching some bozo throw rocks and call his mom.

When I go home, my parents are just as excited as the teachers are, proclaiming this a great moment in history.

"You gotta meet this guy, get your picture taken with him. You'll care about this one day," my mother says.

What magic spell did Gushue cast to charm everyone I've ever known, even my own parents? Was it an enthralling, enchanted glint of light off his medallion, hanging from his neck like an ancient rosary of a dark wizard's long-forgotten religion? Or was it some magic incantation, a spell disguised as some local aphorism, shushed into the flip phone at the end of the session? Why didn't his spell work on me? Maybe I didn't hear his magical remarks, maybe my glasses deflected the moonstruck glint of his accursed laurel, maybe I'm immune to the charms of the curlomancer's wicked ways.

An airport employee had also been charmed into adoration of Team Gushue and it became rumoured, then known, that the winning team's flight home from the Olympics would arrive at three in the morning and that Gushue would even be wearing the medal.

"We have to go," my mother says.

On a cold February night, I'm dragged from the comfort of my own home in the wee hours of the morning, by my own parents no less, to see Lord Gushue in the flesh. We were not alone at the airport. A crowd of hundreds, nay, thousands gathered to see Gushue and his medal, from family members to reporters to one sleep-deprived child who would rather be at home. Those sliding doors at the top of the Arrivals escalator open, and out walk Team Gushue in matching red-and-white nationalist outfits, with their freshly minted bling hanging from their necks.

Mark and Jamie, move out of the way! Lord Gushue walks among us mere mortals. Does he have the flip phone with him? Will his embodied presence allow us to take photos with him? Can he be photographed, or is he too powerful to even be documented? Lord Gushue makes his way through the crowd slowly and everyone acts as if we've never seen a man before, every father, boyfriend and husband Pillsbury'd and pitiful in Gushue's shadow. There's rumours spreading through the crowd that if you touch the gold, you'll be granted eternal youth. The medals have a hole in the middle, which sparks yet another rumour to murmur through the crowd that the Olympic committee made this year's oddly shaped medal in a conspiracy to defraud Newfoundland of any respect we could possibly incur from this fortuitous occasion.

At last, Lord Gushue is near me.

"Brad, can my son get his photo with you? He loves you," my mom says, prompting a sleepily raised eyebrow from me.

I get the photo.

Lord Gushue walks on.

We leave the airport but this is only the beginning of Lord Gushue's Reign of Terror. First, he seizes the education system. A painting of Lord Gushue is placed in the hallway of our school for us all to regard with a sense of reverence and bow down to in the mornings before class begins. Then he comes for our land. A new suburban development is to be forged in Lord Gushue's honour, with the streets being named after the Lord himself, and his minions Mark and Jamie. Then he seized the infrastructure, with a new megahighway interchange to be built bearing his name and the evergreen highway signs to be emblazoned with the sigil of the Dark Lord: a cartoon curling rock. And these are merely the facts. Rumours abound through the city that the crushing grasp of his reach is growing larger, unbridled.

"He just bought the house down the street and he's going to rent it out to university students and curling protégés."

"Brad Gushue is going to open an ice cream shoppe, but he doesn't call it 'ice cream,' he calls it 'fro-yo.'" His ability to speak in such tongues was granted to him by that gold medallion, no doubt.

"I heard he's going to open a shoe store called Gu-Shoes."

Every now and then, Lord Gushue will bless his adoring public with a meet-and-greet, to commemorate the opening of a new cellphone store in the mall or to celebrate Canada Day at the Rooms. I go and see him at all of these events, wary that he will soon seize the means of production and that the province will fall into a Gushue nation-state.

It goes without saying that every Newfoundlander enrolled in curling lessons immediately after Gushue won gold, with the sport quickly becoming an essential part of our provincial identity. My elementary school first trains us to play Newfoundland's new favourite traditional pastime in the gymnasium, foisting a dollar-store Swiffer into every hand, and, most egregiously, pairs of thick wool socks strained over our shoes, Nan's knitwear being the perfect material to simulate sliding on ice across the hardwood gym floor. A sorry excuse for curling lessons, with dozens of children tempting fate against a concussion. I put accident and injury lawyers on speed-dial in my In-Case-of-Emergency hand-me-down flip phone. After realizing that not even Nan's socks could make the garish gym feel like a curling rink, the school drags the lot of us down to the RE/MAX Centre to learn how to really curl.

I don't want to be at the RE/MAX Centre. I don't want to be a curler. I don't care about any of this. Ice is too slippery for me, and needless physical activity is too strenuous. I loiter alongside the rink lanes, trying to look involved without having to actually do anything, alternately sizing up the Swiffers and straining to lift the rocks. It's not long before the faculty wises up to this and forces me on to the ice.

Indeed, there is a distinct pleasure in sliding a rock across the ice and watching it float away from me with an eager hope that it will land on what is deemed to be the right part of the ice. Maybe I could grow to like this.

This momentary bliss only lasts so long, as in the foolish ecstasy of throwing rocks, I rush to grab another rock, blindly throwing my hand towards where they're stored. What I don't see is one of my buddies putting a rock back there at the same time because "it doesn't handle quite right" for this burgeoning curloisseur. What I don't see is my fingers getting jammed between two rocks, but I sure as hell feel it.

I burst into tears in the middle of the curling rink. The teachers rush around me.

Yes, I can still bend my fingers. No, I don't think they're broken. Yes, it hurts. Yes, I ruined everyone's time at the curling rink. After assessing my fingers and determining my response to be an overreaction, the teachers reprimand me.

"Boys your age don't cry," the principal says to me while I'm in detention. "Men don't cry."

"But Gushue cried," I say, thinking of the painting in the hall.

The principal says nothing, doesn't bother with my rebuttal, already moved on to try to mould another detention inmate to fit his narrow prescription of how a person should be.

I never curl again.

As the years passed and the seasons of the Earth repeated themselves, the influence of Lord Gushue waned over the people of Newfoundland. The Team Gushue Highway opened to little fanfare. The highway too was influenced by his sorcery, as it connected Kenmount Road, the great road which contained all matters of commercial delights, to the distant and foreign community of Mount Pearl, a treacherous zone that previously existed only in the shadowy recesses of the minds of the damned. Gushue's diabolic influence briefly grew in power again in 2016 when the Tim Hortons Brier came to Newfoundland, the largest sporting event for curling named after a now-defunct brand of tobacco. Lest you think Lord Gushue was merely an arm of Big Tobacco this entire time, it turns out that most people are unaware of the event's cancerous origins.

Although Gushue won the Brier and obtained Olympic glory again, our province was no longer seized with the same sort of delirious fervour that gripped us after his first Olympic victory. Some remained entranced by his hypnotic rocks, breathlessly reporting to a radio audience of dozens his every goal and fumble. However, many had grown used to his tricks, scrolling past his highlight reels on our Facebooks, Instagrams and Twitters. But still, when I drive down Team Gushue Highway or pass by a Swiffer picker upper, I think of being a confused young boy, eyes still wet from tears, being told that men don't cry, all while under the watchful eye of a painting of a man, a champion, crying into a phone far, far away.

you-cee

SOBIA SHAHEEN SHAIKH

The wind hissed and swirled around her. Dust hit her face and burned her eyes, despite the thick, goggle-like leopard-print sunglasses she wore. Oh, wow, she thought, good thing it's sunny out today.

She didn't remember the wind being so fierce when she was last here, twenty years ago. It had always been a wind tunnel, just outside the University Centre.

You-Cee, they called it, where she huddled among other students, and sometimes staff, staring at her boots. She was impatient those days, waiting for the bus to show, proudly displaying "Avalon U—University Centre" across the electronic banner on its forehead—with its engine running and smoke bellowing out the pipe at the back. A gaggle of ill-dressed students waiting outside until the bus driver picked up his coffee from the second floor. Shamila still didn't understand how they could stand there, wearing thin T-shirts and unbuttoned coats, their breath forming tiny ice crystals.

The You-Cee was always talking, laughing, wafting smells of pizza and Thai food. And now, well, it looked so lonely. The window-lined Business Centre beside it still shone like a new, shiny, gold-plated blister, but the face of the building was crumbling. She remembered when they opened it, the same year that students deliriously protested tuition hikes. The same year that the angry, purple hives appeared on her face, as she fretted she had to go back home empty-handed, without a degree. When she heard that tuition had tripled, she had felt ashamed and betrayed; she barely left her bed. Shamila hid out for weeks before she let her fear succumb to rage and marched herself to the rally.

She blushed as she remembered her face on the front page of the newspaper, underneath the headline "International Students Fight Back," looking enraged against the backdrop of the Business Centre, and as if she had adorned her face with the purple-red paint of the university hues. Her parents would have been embarrassed if they had seen it—"Shamila! How could you be so reckless?" they would have tutted—but she was proud of that picture, hives and all. She looked up and down at the Business Centre, tilting her head, judgmental.

"And now, now you look so . . . forlorn. Is that the right word?" she asked the Business Centre aloud, aware that she was ever the international student, wondering whether she had her English terms well in hand.

"The gold plating has been chipped," she said, wryly, out loud, turning back to catch a flare of light on the shank of the once-new, rotting Business building.

She turned her attention back to her new workplace. The You-Cee had always been her favourite place. She made memories there: drinking coffee, studying, daydreaming, slurping her soup, hauling psych texts day after day without opening them, missing home, and then finding home. She went to the You-Cee after the roads were cleared from Snowmageddon. She'd run out of food—she always ran out of food in those days—but all the stores were locked down. She was lucky she braved scurrying through walls of snow, because when she arrived at the food court in the You-Cee, she found a party there. Students from all over the world, international students, feeding each other with thermoses of stew and curry, loud. Chen's face flushing after he pecked Nandi on the cheek. Pinky shaking the white fluff off her long, flowy hair like a goddess on a runway. Sharing bread, giddiness.

She could still remember savouring Oyo's homemade pastries. She closed her eyes as she slowly tasted the doughy-deliciousness, and thought, I am never going back home. This is where I belong.

A gust of wind thrashed the front door of the You-Cee like an uninvited visitor, nudging her out of warm memories. She paused. The You-Cee was also the place where she had fallen depressed. Well, at least I won't bump into Dr. Pinker now, and she thought about the last time she had seen him. He was known to be a "perv," to prey on his students' desires to be seen and validated, and he had tried his luck with her.

Shamila had heard the rumours. Dr. Pinker was someone to watch out for. He'd had been in relationships with students, but they were all "consenting," "adults," grad students who were on the rise and were "benefiting" from his attention. But she never thought much about it. Not until she nearly collided with him that day, rushing to the campus store to get a last-minute gift for her ammi before her flight back home. The second floor of the You-Cee was unusually quiet, and he had been turning the corner, his footsteps echoing in the empty hallway. They came face to face, and she nervously dropped her purse.

"Hullo, Sha-mi-laaah," he had crooned, with an emphasis

wrongly placed on the last syllable of her name.

Ordinarily, she would have brushed past him, and said hello, and gone on her way. But his voice, the slow and deliberate clicks of the silver pen he always had in his hand, made her stop in her tracks.

And when Dr. Pinker nonchalantly, as if he was entitled to, slipped his hand over her shoulder and through the boat-shaped neckline of her pink shirt, reached in to graze her breasts, she recoiled.

And she wasn't having it—she marched up to the provost's office shaking and unannounced. The secretary must have been shocked, because she ushered her into the provost's office without a word. Shamila felt fortunate that she had done a research assistantship with the provost months before—she knew that most students, and especially a Pakistani international student, a female psychology student to boot, would not have been able to attend the provost's chamber.

But she knew the provost, or at least she thought she understood her. Weeks before the run-in with Dr. Pinker, Shamila had a curious encounter with the provost, who'd come into the conference room where Shamila had been stationed, shut the door and just cried. Bewildered, Shamila asked her boss what happened, and out came a torrent of frustration about sexism and expletives she had not expected to hear. She had no idea that someone, a woman, so powerful, so composed—so Canadian and white—could be subject to the sort of degradation that Shamila thought was reserved only for people like her.

After the provost blew her nose into a crumpled Kleenex from her pocket, she looked up at Shamila and said crisply: "Well, that's that. And we soldier on to live and fight another day."

They'd never spoken about it again, and the provost went back to sending her emails in the middle of the night, issuing orders.

When she'd gone to counselling years later, at her ex-girlfriend's insistence, her counsellor suggested that Dr. Pinker had been grooming her. She wasn't sure but she remembered his intrusive gazes, his questions. She had thought they were becoming friends.

Dr. Pinker had seemed so genuinely interested in her bubbly and pragmatic outlook, as he called it. He told her, "I've never met someone as put together and yet so intensely vulnerable."

"Fascinating," he would say, looking at her intently until she squirmed. "You're not like the others, are you?"

"Did you tell Maya about our meeting? Was she jealous?"

"Did you sleep in the same bed?"

"What do you mean, discriminating, do you mean racist?" he asked incredulously.

"Did you and Oyo get, well, um, intimate?"

"In your culture, are girls fond of other girrrlls?" rolling his Rs.

If she told him how she felt about something, he'd ask, "Which part of the body does that experience resonate with?"

He would insistently ask, "Show me, where."

But then, well, he was an academic. And academics seemed to be a bit . . . intense, she thought. So she had chalked up her strange conversations to difference.

But after he'd reached inside her blouse she went directly to the provost's office and told her story. The provost listened intently, in silence, except for the sounds of uncomfortable shifting in her leather seat. When Shamila was finished, the provost said sombrely: "Thank you for sharing this. I believe you, and I'm sorry. You can be assured that we'll investigate." And then Shamila was dismissed.

Shamila left her office feeling heard, but didn't have much faith that one complaint from a brown student would make a difference. Yet it seemed to have. Amazingly, Dr. Pinker had been reprimanded publicly and then he just kind of faded away. She wondered what had happened to all those women he had harmed, those whispers she had heard.

As she willed the memories away, her sky-blue scarf was taken by the wind, and she bent to grab it. She shook the dust and paper debris off frenziedly and stuffed the scarf in her pocket.

How did I end up back here now, she thought.

After COVID-19 and the disaster of the megadam project, the economy tanked, and the government pulled all in-person public education programs and services, and all the programs went completely virtual. The province went bankrupt and Avalon U was defunded. Only Atlantic College remained open, at reduced capacity, and the Labrador Campus was eventually revived and taken over by Innu and Inuit philanthropists. She remembered when she got news that Avalon was purchased by Raeks University, a completely online institution in Northern Ontario: a "merger," they called it. That was the year she applied for her MBA, four years after she graduated. She was devastated, heartbroken, and she vowed she would never come back to Avalon U. Instead, she moved off the island to go to UNB in Saint John.

Best decision I ever made, she said. That was where she met and married gruff-but-big-hearted Dennie. Yup, I thought I would never be back here, looking up at the glass doors, but here I am.

Dennie didn't want to move to St. John's with her, at least, they said, not yet. "If this job suits yuh, and you're happy, I'll come to you in a'ear." But not yet. Not yet, not yet, not yet: she heard a definite echo in her ears. She looked around, but there was no one there.

And here she was. Right now. All the buildings had been closed, except for the medical school, the You-Cee and the Administration Building, she had been told, when she enquired. And now she was back, as a brand-new staff at the You-Cee, to rebuild and reignite an in-person campus, after a wealthy benefactor, an Avalon alumnus, had invested money in the university real estate.

She pushed her hair back, around her ears, poked her finger on the bridge of her glasses, and leaned forward. She used all of her strength to open the glass door heavy with the wind; she grunted as it yielded.

When she got in the building, she took off her sunglasses and peered around at the bottom of the stairs.

Shamila trekked up a flight of stairs. But when she got to the first landing, she remembered that there'd been an elevator. "There's not a soul in here," she said out loud. She thought she heard a shimmer of a laugh. She looked around again. A faraway noise, something in the air vents. The corridors had holes cut in the walls, covered with Tyvek attached with silver strips of tape. They have a lot of work still to do here, she thought. As she walked past, the Tyvek rippled slightly, her body displacing the still, stale air, like something breathing in the walls.

She found the elevator and pressed the button; it lit up. She got in and walked out the doors to what had once been the Student Centre.

"Helloooo," she said. Empty and echoey. No students here. She used the pass key she had been given at the Administration Building and let herself into her new office.

It looks efficient and neat, she thought. A desk and chair, bookshelves, a phone, a computer. Someone had unpacked her boxes of books and stacked three other boxes labelled

"SK, Personal" off to the right. It smelled of cleaning fumes, intermingled with dust. At least it had a big window.

"And," she said, "I guess I'm ready to work."

She dropped into the plush green rolling office chair and wriggled into the cushion. She turned on the button on the computer underneath her desk and smiled in anticipation as the opening music played. There was a single flower on the right side of her computer. A tulip, a cranberry-red tulip. It was beautiful, alive, and lonely. This. This was not what she was expecting at all. After the feelings of desolation she'd encountered at the You-Cee, and the perfunctory coolness at the orientation in the Administration Building, this gift seemed out of place. Who put it there?

Just then, Dennie called. "Well, how is it," they demanded. "Are any of your co-workers Black or brown?"

Shamila laughed at the familiarity of their question, "No, Dennie. I literally haven't seen anyone at all. But the office is nice, and it brings back good memories . . . The office seems kind of homey, and they even sent me an office-warming tulip and vase. It's this strange cranberry-red colour, almost feels like it's glowing."

"A tulip? In Septemba'? That's kind of sweet, welcoming," Dennie said. "Send me a picture."

Shamila said, "I miss you."

Dennie groaned, "Yeah, me too. But the shelter jus got some new funding for the trans sex-worker project, so I got lotsa work to do. Call me lata', when y'get home?"

Shamila hung up the phone, stared at the flower, "I guess it's just you and me, kiddo." She thought she heard a slight giggle and she looked around for an air vent, maybe some breeze jostling the window blinds. She was learning not to trust her own ears. *This place is already getting to me, and it's not even* been three hours, she thought. She turned on the computer and began to develop her work plan to make sure that the You-Cee Student Centre was ready to welcome in-person students again.

The next morning was a bit cloudier, just the way she remembered St. John's, and as she parked her Volvo outside the You-Cee, Shamila glanced up at the window she thought was her office. She'd left the lights on, she didn't quite know what prompted her to do that. She was usually so energy-conscious, especially since oil production and sales had stalled around the world. But she'd been nervous when she left after her first workday, and the corridors were empty and they seemed to stretch on, one of the overhead lights was burnt out, and another light was hanging on, buzzing, at the end of the hall, near the stairwell. Bzzzzz, click, click, click.

She realized when she got home to her new condo-apartment by Quidi Vidi Lake that she hadn't sent Dennie that picture of her tulip. As she took the elevator up to her office, she made a mental note to take a picture straight away, before the flower faded.

But when she got to her office, the tulip had been replaced by a rose, a single cranberry-red rose, with the same glowing quality. "Hmmmff," she said. "That's weird, it's the same colour." So she took a picture of it with her cellphone.

Look what I got this morning, she texted with a smiley-face emoji. As she studied the picture on her phone, she could see that the rose seemed faded, less vibrant somehow. Maybe I need to clean the lens on my camera, she thought.

Dennie texted back, Hi love. Can't see anything, it's blank. Ttys. xxxx

She'd try again later after she cleaned her phone lens. She turned on her computer, paused. Instead of tinkering with the document, she called the Dean of Administrative Services. He picked up the phone on the first ring.

"Good morning, Dr. Coleman, this is Shamila . . ."

"Gerald," he said, perfunctorily.

"Oh yes. Gerald."

Gerald-call-me-Gerald had spoken sparsely and seemed distracted when they last met, even when he was looking directly towards her.

She continued: "I'm just wondering if you have a list of staff who have access to the You-Cee? I haven't yet met anyone, and I want to know who works here so I can introduce myself later today."

"Yes, I think I can do that, let me look," he said, clacking away.

"Ah," she paused. "Okay, does the list include caretaking staff?"

Gerald said, "Mm-hmm, yup."

"Great, thank you, that's exactly what I want."

"We'll see you later today, you remember the tunnels under the building? You can take those, I'll send some directions by email."

"Mm-hmm," she said. "Yes, I'll be by this afternoon to discuss the plan for reopening and the Centre and its staffing needs. Does three still work?" She paused.

"You're in my calendar," he replied.

"Great, see you then."

At two-thirty, she shut off her computer and began to get her cashmere wrap on. Before closing the door, she glanced back at the office, and the rose looked brighter, appeared to shimmer.

"Yup," she said out loud, "you are definitely beautiful, a delight. But I'm off to see Gerald-call-me-Gerald," she said to nobody.

She left her office with map in hand, down to the basement to join the tunnel to the Administration Building. The tunnel still smelled like asbestos, and she was glad that she had brought her mask. The familiar oozing green still lined parts of the tunnels, and there was water seeping up from the cracks in the concrete floors. The pipes loudly shivered, and she heard click, click, click behind her. Footsteps? When she looked behind her, down the hall, there was no one there.

"Yup, this place is still gross, and yup, I'm losing my mind." She picked up the pace, still looking over her shoulder. Mental note: do not ever take the tunnels again. The tunnels should have been closed long before she had been a student.

The green ooze on the walls seemed to crawl across the cinderblocks. This is the last time, she panted, but she was almost there, so she kept going.

She sighed relief when she got to Gerald-call-me-Gerald's office. The receptionist, a tall, burly man no more than twenty-five years old, smiled and offered Shamila some tea. And that was when she realized that she had been holding her breath and exhaled.

The meeting was uneventful, and Gerald-call-me-Gerald seemed pleased with Shamila's work and staffing plan.

After the meeting, despite the light rain, Shamila ventured out the front door, and instead of going back to her office, made straight for her car parked outside the You-Cee and went home to take a warm shower.

For the next four days, she was gifted a new flower every day—a hyacinth, which smelled divine. An iris. A chrysanthemum and then a larkspur. She had to look up the name of the larkspur—I'm beginning to get to know my flowers at least, she thought. All the same iridescent cranberry-red.

"Curiouser and curiouser," she said. She couldn't remember which movie that was from, but the exclamation seemed fitting.

After that fifth day, she organized an office-warming party. "It was sweet," she told Dennie that evening; "everyone seems so lovely, and yes, I have racialized co-workers"—before Dennie could ask again.

She had made a point to meet other staff at the You-Cee earlier in the week and had even bumped into Mizz Penney when she came in early one morning. Mizz Penney, the caretaker, a fifty-something woman with blond hair from a box. Warm and effusive, she spoke quickly.

Shamila told her about the flowers and asked if she had seen anyone in the building. Mizz Penney, said, "Isn't that interesting," paused to think about it, and then in a sing-songy way, "I don't know nudding about it. Maybe someone's sweet on you? Dr. Coleman is single, and he swings by sometimes."

"No, I don't think so." She hesitated. "But who else would have access to my office? I'm not worried or anything," Shamila said worriedly, with a faux-brightness. "I love the flowers, and there's a charm in not knowing." Shamila looked straight at Mizz Penney, narrowing her eyes. "But it's strange, and I almost thought it might be you."

"No, missus," said Mizz Penney. "But I'll look out fer ya. Five in the morning, I comes in."

Shamila began to count her days by the flowers she received, by their wafty fragrance, their mesmerizing details—the smoothness, the dimples, that shimmery-glimmery-cranberry-red delightfulness. She spent hours alone, except on the days she met her building-mates for lunch or coffee. And somehow, she barely felt lonely, glancing up at the flower of the day. Sometimes the blossom seemed to tip towards her as the day drained away, as if it were heliotropic and she were the sun. She still had no idea who was sending them, and she knew she should be creeped out, but the flowers kept her company.

Several flowers later—night-blooming jasmine, fireweed, lupins, baby's breath and sunflowers—she had her first interviews to hire her staff, student assistants to help her with readying the You-Cee's opening scheduled later that term. Some were graduate, some undergraduate, and as she did the perfunctory questions—What is your biggest strength? What is your biggest challenge and how will you overcome it?—she stifled many irritated yawns. It wasn't that the students weren't good candidates, but they weren't *the* candidate. The one who really understood this place, who could see the possibilities and enjoy the quirks of the Centre.

It was 4:25 p.m. and she was deflated, waiting for the last candidate. Although the woman's résumé was not very strong, she had a lot of administrative experience. She had been an Avalon student on and off for several years, but there were many gaps in her record. Judging from her student number, Shamila figured that she might have started university five years after Shamila herself had left. She had re-registered at Avalon this year, and judging by the courses she took, was hoping to finish year three of her Bachelor of Commerce degree in person.

When Shamila looked up, she almost gasped. The student looked very young, instead of the forty-something that she had expected. Her dead-straight almost-black hair was back in a ponytail that almost shimmered, and her turquoise-blue tank top seemed to have taken on the translucency of her pale skin. She was very plain—and yet her features had a haughtiness. Her eyes sparkled a little, almost misty.

But you look like you belong here, Shamila said silently to herself. The flowers seemed to have perked up, as if they had heard her thoughts.

"Hullo," the woman said. "I'm Kalie, I applied for the assistant position?"

"Yes, glad to meet you, I'm Shamila." She offered her hand, and Kalie tentatively took it, and for a moment, she looked like she was in pain, concentrating hard. Shamila tried not to drop her cold and clammy hand, and thought to herself, she must be really nervous. Even I'm nervous.

She began to ask Kalie questions about her skills, her strengths and weaknesses, what she was most excited about. Kalie's answers were terse, edgy, cryptic: yes, no, I'm not sure. More annoying was that at the corner of her eye, Shamila could swear the flower beside her was pulsing in rhythm with whatever Kalie said. The more agitated Kalie seemed to become, the more the flower brightened, fading in the pauses or when Kalie held her breath. Shamila felt an overwhelming compulsion to look at the flower, but to look away from Kalie seemed unprofessional.

So she determinedly locked her gaze with the woman and took another tack: she stopped the interview questions, and she said, "Kalie, I'm sensing you are feeling uncomfortable. Help me make a decision about this assistantship position. Tell me about why you would like to work here and why you think I should hire you."

Kalie squirmed in her seat, but in a clear voice, suddenly devoid of hesitation, she said, "I belong to this place. I am this place. The You-Cee is very important to students like me."

Shamila stammered, "I, yes, mm-hmm, the Student Centre is important. And that's why we need students like you to help us build this Centre up . . ."

Kalie interrupted: "Students like me who have been abandoned. Students who were promised protection, care, and then just dropped."

Shamila said, "I can understand how you feel. The Student Centre was full of life when I was last here . . . We need a new Student Centre, which is why I'm here. Tell me, I see from your application that you have done some administrative work at the College. Can you tell me about that?"

Kalie said, "No, that's not what I mean." Now Shamila was getting agitated, and her eyes darted back and forth from Kalie to her phone. Out of the corner of her eye she noticed the cranberry-red sunflower seemed to be trembling, blaring like the neon lights she saw down on George Street so many years ago. Shamila turned to look at the flower sharply, and then back to the young woman who, Shamila felt, was projecting herself into the flower. But that's absurd, she thought.

Shamila gripped the edge of her desk with a finger and thumb. "Kalie, what *is it* that you mean?"

Kalie's eyes blazed as she looked at Shamila, opened her mouth and closed it, and then magically seemed to centre herself. Kalie responded flatly, "I took care of people at the College, I took care of people's projects. I assisted in whatever ways I was asked. I am good at helping people with things that they care about, and I care about this Centre. I want to help you rebuild it."

Shamila let out a breath, and said, "Thank you, Kalie. Do you have any final questions for me, about the Centre, about how I work?"

"I think I know everything I need to know," she said. "I look forward to working with you soon. Thank you again." And she walked out the door.

Shamila, sank back into her chair. She dialled Dennie's number. "Hi Dennie . . . no, nothing's wrong, I just needed to hear your voice."

"What's uhp, darlin," they asked gently over the speakerphone, more like an invitation than a question.

"I just don't know if I can do this, I'm getting weirded out by this place, I'm so lonely, I'm hearing things, clicky things and creaks, and I don't know. The only thing lovely about this place is my memories, and the flowers."

Dennie laughed, "Yeah, and even when you send me pix of those, all I get is faded-out blanks, so I'm beginning to think you're making the flowers up!"

Dennie continued softly, "Luv, y'wanna come home?"

Shamila looked at her flower and sighed, "No, not yet. I think I found my assistant, intense and strange, but I think she's right, she'll work out just fine."

"Kalie," she said contemplatively. The flower seemed to have perked up and the heaviness in her office and in her voice left in a swoosh. "But y'know what, I really miss you," she continued. "When can you come and visit? How's the new project going?"

Over the next few weeks, Kalie and Shamila developed a good working rhythm, and the anxiety surrounding their first meeting had all but dissipated. Kalie had been right, she was turning out to be a good support. Sometimes when Shamila sent Kalie an email in the middle of the night, by the next morning, Kalie had already responded. She seemed to understand what was needed, and her work was meticulous. She definitely needed help with writing; she wasn't able to be concise, but that was fine.

Kalie came to the office almost every day, even on days she wasn't scheduled. "I'm just doing my homework, and I have nowhere else to go," she said. Shamila didn't mind and they seemed to enjoy each other's presence.

And so Shamila welcomed her and the beautiful flowers which seemed to have grown even more beautiful and bold, radiant and loved.

One day, on a day when Kalie was scheduled to help with choosing the paint colours for the new Student Centre, she didn't show up. Shamila called her, but there was no answer. Maybe she is not feeling well, Shamila thought.

She decided to take a break and saunter over to see Linda-from-the-second-floor at the newly built Food Services Office.

As she got up from her desk, she thought she heard heavy, sloppy footsteps, click, click, click. Oh maybe that's Kalie? she thought. So she went to the door to greet her, with a wide grin, saying, "Oh there you are! I was a bit, worried, where . . .?"

The question hung in the air.

Shamila gasped as she looked up at a tall, dishevelled, greying man, a man who held a silver pen in his right hand. He clicked and clicked and clicked his pen and held it up to her face.

"Hullo, Sha-mi-laaah," he drawled.

Shamila took a step back and bumped into her door frame. He was older, but it was definitely him.

"Oh, come on, Shamila," he taunted. "You haven't forgotten me, now have you? Or did you think your one complaint would have made any difference?"

"Dr. Pinker?" Shamila stammered.

"Yes, that's me." Putting his chin up even higher. "Dr. Pinker, in the fleshhh."

"B-but why are you here? How are you here?" she asked.

"Why don't you welcome me into your new Student Centre, into your office?" he said.

"Dr. Pinker," she said, disengaging her back from the door frame. She took a step back and tried to compose herself, "Wha-what are you doing he-here?"

"Well, I do have other business. I am the head of the Business Centre, opening next month, just before your Student Centre. But when I heard that you had taken a post here, I thought, well, well, well, isn't that lovely, what a nice time for a reacquaintance."

Shamila moved back into her doorway. Every time she

stepped back, Pinker advanced like a sinister dance partner.

Shamila opened her eyes wide. "What do you want from me?" she asked, stepping back towards her desk.

"I wanted to assure you that I was fine. After you did your little song-and-dance, and that blasted woman-feminist-nothingness of a provost charged me with sexual harassment, I was . . . well, I was fine." He took a sharp inhale. "But then when the business of the merger became public, just like that, they took me back. I was reinstated, and nobody asked any questions. I was made provost of the Business faculty, and now, well, let's just say I've done very well for myself."

Pinker leaned in and she felt his breath on her face. "And so you see, my girl, nothing you have done has ever made an ounce of difference.

"I've been watching you. And I know you felt it, you heard me.

"Oh, I hate this building, this place freaks me out. But because I hate you more, I came here. So, for you, my girl, I put my disgust for this place aside, and came in through the doors."

Shamila edged back, baby steps, and tried to close the door, but her stalker was too fast and darted in her office. He leaned into her body, and she was pinned by the desk. She could feel his chest against hers as he smirked, enjoying her fear. Shamila turned her head towards her desk, hoping to grab her cellphone.

His eyes darted to the phone, and then all of a sudden, Pinker jerked up and recoiled. He gasped.

Shamila grabbed her phone and followed his gaze. The crimson calla lily looked as if it had grown three times as large as it had been moments before. The bell of the lily seemed ready to fire.

He said, "WHERE did you get that flower? Is SHE here?" He looked like he wanted to run, but couldn't; his impulse to flee suddenly thwarted, and his feet seemed to be frozen in place.

Shamila composed herself and began to dial 911.

She heard a sound from her office door, and when she looked up, she saw Kalie. Shamila saw Kalie, but a Kalie she had never seen before. Her eyes looked feverish, wet with tears, her face angry and contorted.

"Get out, you vile man, LEAVE!" Kalie shrilled.

Pinker began to whimper, "I thought—I thought—I thought I . . . I . . . You can't be . . . you're supposed to be . . ."

His menacing look was replaced with shame and fear.

Pinker made a run for it, and Kalie thundered, "No. You should not have returned."

As Pinker scrambled down the stairwell, Kalie began to move her hands in small circles, in unison, and began humming a high-pitched, ethereal melody that Shamila had never heard but felt familiar, like the faint sound she thought she heard when the flowers were pulsing. The circles that Kalie made with her hands became circles she made with her wrist, and then up and down her body as she raised her arms and flung her neck back, as if she were channelling all of her being into her arms.

And then Shamila saw them, the glittery-red petals of the calla lily, coming off the flowers in her office. And then more petals from sunflowers, roses, larkspur, baby's breath, too numerous to count, too numerous to name. They circled Kalie's head like a tornado, and they themselves began to hum.

As Pinker ran down the stairs, he yelled, "No, no, no!" the petals spinning around Kalie's head, with tornado speed, a red blur filling Shamila's office, gushing out the door, down the corridor.

The petals descended the stairs and followed Dr. Pinker in an ominous vortex, humming and whirling until they reached him. The strange force Kalie wielded, the gleaming flower petals, her avatars, were lifting, pushing, conveying him the doors of the You-Cee, while he tried to swat them away as if they were a swarm of ravenous locusts.

Kalie's eyes glowed and her chanting voice bellowed and echoed through the corridors, "You do not belong here, you will never belong to this place. I do, we do, all those that you and other men-and-women-without-care harmed and abandoned, we belong to this Centre.

"Begone!"

And Kalie and her glittery flower petals pushed him out the door, and the door slammed shut, heavy with the wind.

Shamila ran to the window in the corridor, and saw Pinker running, out past the You-Cee bus stop. Shamila looked sharply back at Kalie and opened her mouth, but no words came out.

They heard a grinding screech of the brakes of a city bus. Out the window, they saw Pinker, unmoving, in front of a bus with the words "Avalon U—University Centre" across the electronic banner on its forehead. The crimson petals, no longer bright and animate, merged with the man's blood, fanning out onto the pavement.

"Ka-Kalie," Shamila turned to see her assistant and shook as she whispered, "Who are you . . ."

"I am You-Cee, and the people the university abandoned. I am tied to this place, and so are you."

They heard the sirens below, and Shamila glanced down at the rushing paramedics.

When she turned back, Kalie was gone. She slumped against the wall, dazed, ready to cry. The phone rang.

She scrambled and pressed the answer button on her phone. "Dennie," she said. "Please come, I need you."

She hung up, gathered her things, and left the office.

the city wears thin

MATTHEW HOLLETT

Sorry about all the scaffolding, Vivian says as she opens the door. Scott's having his siding redone. She picks up some mail from the floor and deposits it on an oval table in the hallway. You can leave your shoes on. Just knock off the sawdust.

So he's your cousin? says Fiona.

Once removed, says Vivian. More like an uncle, really. Come in, the kitchen's in back.

Fiona and Noah follow her down the high-ceilinged hallway. Noah runs his hand over a heavy mahogany banister as they pass the staircase, then lingers at the entrance to the darkened living room. Light from a street lamp gleams through the scaffolding in the window, illuminating surfaces in the room: a steamer trunk used as a coffee table, a knickknacked mantlepiece, and a colourful glass cabinet projecting out from the wall.

Is that a pinball machine? Noah says as he catches up.

It is, Vivian says. Scott's a bit of an eBay fiend. She flicks a switch and the kitchen brightens. A narrow, cluttered table and three wooden chairs are cramped against one wall. There's a gurgling noise that sounds like a river running under the house, and it takes Noah a moment to realize that it's coming from the fridge. Muddy boot prints mar the linoleum floor. The room smells overripe.

No one's living here right now, says Vivian as she opens the refrigerator. The workers just stash their lunches in the fridge. Want a beer?

Always, says Noah, as he examines the wilted herbs on the windowsill.

Just water for me, says Fiona. I drained at least half a bottle of red at the gallery. I can't tell if this headache is from the wine or the heat. She settles into one of the kitchen chairs and pushes a bowl of withered bananas to the far corner of the table. Fruit flies twiddle out of the bowl.

It's been a wickedly humid summer here. Vivian twists the caps off two beers. Tap water okay?

Oh, sure, says Fiona. So where's your cousin, anyway?

El Salvador, says Vivian. Or Ecuador. Which one has the Galápagos?

Oh, I've always wanted to go there, says Noah. It's like Jurassic Park in miniature. The beaches are covered in iguanas and the giant tortoises live to be a hundred.

Scott posted a video of blue-footed boobies, Vivian says as she places a glass of water in front of Fiona. His friends keep commenting that they're reporting it for inappropriate content.

So what does your cousin do, asks Fiona, to fund his lavish lifestyle of pinball and travel porn?

Let me guess, Noah says. Adult film director.

Close. He's an ocean sciences prof. He studies the mating habits of sea cucumbers.

Well, cheers to that, says Noah. Fiona holds up her water and they clink bottles against the glass.

We should say *sociable*! says Vivian. Always a pleasure to welcome fellow Haligonians to my adopted island. Especially ones who appreciate a good cheese plate.

We really destroyed that, didn't we?

You know it's a good opening when you forget to look at the art. Vivian leans against the fridge. She presses the cold beer bottle against her forehead.

Speaking of sea cucumbers, says Fiona. Maybe your cousin would've enjoyed those balloon animal paintings.

Oh, I think Scott gets enough soggy phallic symbols through his research.

Soggy is the perfect word for ... wait, do you know the artist? asks Fiona.

No, not really. We have a hundred friends in common, says Vivian, so I see him every time I open Facebook. In the "people you may know." But we somehow haven't met.

Oh good, says Fiona. I might go on a tirade.

I didn't think they were that bad, says Noah. The balloon shark chasing the balloon clownfish was funny.

Yes, but you love that campy stuff, says Fiona. He watches *Mars Attacks!* about once a week, she says, rolling her eyes at Vivian.

It's a cult classic! says Noah, throwing his arms wide with some restraint, so as not to spill his beer. They make the Martians' brains explode by *yodelling*.

What did you think, Vivian?

I've seen some landscapes by the same artist that I really liked, says Vivian. But this kitschy stuff not so much.

Kitsch I can appreciate, says Fiona. But balloon animals? It's just Jeff Koons fan-wankery. Pop art should be subversive. This was all punchline, there was no risk in it.

It's like cheese, says Noah. There's cheesy cheese, and then there's good cheese. Like that brie.

Exactly. This was cheese without depth. It was like Kraft Singles hung on the wall.

That would be a pretty good art show.

One of our friends in Halifax made a big window mosaic, says Fiona, out of those jam packets you get at diners. Strawberry and marmalade and grape. She hung hundreds of them in a grocery store window, with the light shining through like stained glass. This was at Pete's Frootique.

Oh, I love that place, says Vivian. That sounds gorgeous.

For the first few days it was, says Noah. Then all the jam turned grey. It was pretty unappetizing.

They made her take it down early, says Fiona. I haven't had jam since.

Do you miss Halifax? asks Noah.

Sometimes. St. John's is not that different a city. Weatherwise, or jobwise. But at the same time it's *so* different.

How so?

The people, I think. I didn't grow up here, so it feels fresh. And it works the other way around, like sometimes it feels like I'm more interesting here? As if people like to meet me. Is that silly?

We liked to meet you, says Fiona. You're a good person to meet.

Thanks. Maybe Halifax is like that too, though, if you're not from there. It's hard to say. I like that St. John's doesn't pretend to be bigger than it is. I like that the harbour is a harbour.

The harbour is a harbour?

Instead of a tourist trap, says Vivian.

Just to be clear, says Noah. Cheesy cheese is bad, but a harboury harbour is good.

Vivian laughs. She brushes dust off the kitchen counter.

Yes, yes, says Fiona. This is the nature of cheese and harbours.

I do miss a good donairy donair, says Vivian.

Fiona suddenly claps her hands together over the fruit bowl. Got one, she says, wiping her hands on her jeans.

Sorry, says Vivian, let's get rid of these fruit flies. She picks up the bowl of brown bananas and opens the door at the back of the kitchen. A surge of hot air nuzzles everyone's ankles.

Fiona and Noah follow Vivian through another set of scaffolds and into the backyard.

The house backs on to a parcel of steep, undeveloped land. Maples loom over the fenced yard, their lower leaves illuminated by the glow from the kitchen window. One tree towers up from near the house and scaffolding juts awkwardly around it. In one corner of the yard, a concrete Buddha wearing a mouldy baseball hat keeps watch over a pair of plastic chairs.

A faint cacophony of traffic tumbles down from the top of the hill. Underlying the traffic, Noah detects a distinct rustling noise.

Vivian dumps the bananas over the back fence. Scott composts back there, she says. I think.

What's that noise? asks Noah. The three of them hold still. Vivian slowly lowers the fruit bowl. Summer air oozes over them like taffy. The rustling is softly persistent, like radio static.

Oh, says Vivian, looking up at the trees. It's the spanworms.

The what? says Fiona.

Spanworms, says Vivian. Little insects that roll up in the leaves. You can hear them munching.

Noah and Fiona squint skyward. Most of the maple leaves are curled into compact tubes.

Weird, Noah says, settling into one of the plastic chairs. Some kind of caterpillar?

More like inchworms, Vivian says. Moth larvae. Sometimes they dangle down on webs like spiders. She ducks back in the kitchen, returning the bowl and re-emerging with a pack of cigarettes. One summer they were so bad, she says, the sidewalks turned black and slippery.

Oh, like . . . what's that word for bug poop? says Noah. Frass.

No, no, says Vivian. From millions of squished worms. They drop down from the trees and people step on them. She holds out the open pack and Fiona accepts a cigarette. Noah declines with a wave of his palm.

A couple of years ago the city tried to get rid of them, Vivian says, by giving the trees pills. They'd drill deep into the tree and put a pill in there and the sap pulled it up, like a bloodstream. Something spanworms didn't like the taste of.

Did it work? asks Fiona.

I don't think so, says Vivian, leaning on the maple tree. It was a pilot project. The flare of her lighter glints off the kitchen window as she lights Fiona's cigarette, then her own.

So you've been in St. John's how many years? Fiona asks.

Five, says Vivian. Four at the university library. Hard to believe.

Seems like it's working, says Noah.

It's mostly working, says Vivian. I moved here with someone who was going to MUN, we split up, I stayed. The job made it easy to stay. I like my boss, she's a powerhouse.

And you have family here?

Oh just Scott, he's been here forever. He's in his forties.

And he's yet to crack the mystery of sea cucumber sex? says Noah.

I don't know if you'd call it sex. They spurt clouds at each other.

He must run into trouble posting those videos on Facebook too, says Fiona.

If you ask me, says Noah, the biggest mystery is why they don't turn into sea pickles. From being so long in the briny deep.

Har har, says Fiona. Although sea pickles does sound more marketable. People eat them, don't they?

Oh yes. Vivian exhales and smoke rises through the maple leaves. They're a delicacy in some places. Dried or deep-fried. Scott could tell you all about it.

Fiona examines some flowers in a raised bed beside the fence. I hear the restaurant scene here is lit, she says.

It's the golden age of locally sourced entrées, says Vivian. Everything comes with chanterelles and seaweed now. Or a sprig of juniper. It's amazing how it's changed just since I've been here. I don't think they've achieved sea-cucumber sushi yet, thankfully.

Those balloon-fish paintings were reminding me of something, says Fiona. And I just realized what it is.

Oh yeah?

Them and the sea cucumbers I guess. They make me think of these incredible glass sea creatures I saw in Scotland.

Oh, those ones you showed me photos of? says Noah.

Yeah, the sea anemones and jellyfish. Just the most exquisite things you've ever seen, you can't even believe they're made of glass. It was at the big museum in Edinburgh. The Blaschka models.

Hold on, says Vivian, this sounds familiar.

They were brothers—or a father and son, I can't remember—who made glass models of marine creatures. For museums and universities, so they could study them. This was before photography, and there was no way to preserve stuff with soft bodies. Jellyfish would just melt in formaldehyde. So they made these super-detailed models in hand-painted glass and wire and sold them all over the world.

And flowers, says Noah. Those famous glass flowers at Harvard.

Oh my god, says Vivian. Scott has one of those!

A flower made of glass?

No not a flower, says Vivian. One of the sea creatures. By the guys who made the flowers. A cucumber I guess, I'm not sure. Or like a cucumber with fins. He showed it to me once, a little purple thing on a wooden stand. It looked really old.

Really? I don't think you can just buy those on eBay.

No, an old friend of his teaches at McGill. They have a collection there but it's been in storage for years, Scott told me the models are basically falling apart. His friend smuggled him a small one as a birthday present. This fluttery purple creature. I remember the label has that beguiling old loopy handwriting.

Oh! says Fiona. I'd really love to see that. They were just astonishing in person.

I'm sure it's in this house. I'd show you, but honestly ... I have no idea where it is. I know he doesn't keep it on display, it's really fragile.

Maybe he keeps it in the fridge, says Noah, with the other pickle specimens.

It's probably upstairs, he has a ton of stuff stored up there. But I wouldn't know where to look.

Too bad, says Fiona. But that's still really cool. She takes a puff of her cigarette and winces.

How's your headache, Fi? says Noah.

I feel like a Martian listening to Slim Whitman, Fiona says, rubbing her temple.

Aw, says Noah. We can head out soon. The washroom's upstairs?

Mm-hmm, one floor up at the end of the hall. Past the barbershop pole.

Barbershop pole?

eBay.

Noah takes Vivian's empty bottle as he goes into the kitchen.

There's more beer in the fridge. Vivian blows smoke away from the open door. Are you guys really taking off? We could go to the Ship, it's just down the hill. There might be music.

Usually we would, but I have an early start tomorrow. It's a very conferency conference.

At least you don't have far to walk. You said your Airbnb is just over on Merrymeeting? I can go with you guys, it's on my way home.

So you live close by? asks Fiona.

Just a few minutes from here. We could've gone to my place. I just realized I had Scott's key on me, and he has this. Vivian flutters her fingers to indicate the backyard, the stackable chairs, the trees.

Scott doesn't mind you using his house?

Oh, I bring in his mail and water the plants, Vivian says. Once a week or so. I should do the plants before we go.

I'm slowly becoming a plant person, says Fiona. A co-worker gave me one for my office. A little pepper plant. And she said if I want peppers, I have to pollinate it myself. By pressing my finger in one of the flowers and touching all the other flowers.

Yeah, you have to spread the pollen around, says Vivian. Did it work?

I haven't tried it yet, laughs Fiona. It feels indecent somehow.

Indecent? Vivian taps her cigarette on the trunk of the maple.

Like what am I doing? Tricking the plant into fucking itself? It feels like some kind of violation.

Well you could always release a bunch of bees in your office.

My office is already full of drones. But that might liven up the place. Hey, watch behind you.

What?

A spider. Hanging there by your ear.

Vivian turns her head. Oh! she says. A spanworm. That's the worst thing about Scott's backyard. Last summer we were out here and one plopped right in my drink.

Maybe it always dreamed of being a tequila worm. Fiona laughs. She peers at the dangling insect. It's kind of cute, she says.

Is it though?

The way it curls up and pokes around. It's like it can't decide if it wants to be a question mark or an exclamation point.

It's going to be an asterisk if it's not careful, says Vivian, holding up her cigarette. I don't know why they bungee jump like that, when they could just huddle in their leaves until they sprout wings.

Are you sure Scott doesn't mind us smoking in the house? says Fiona, following Vivian under the metal bars.

Oh he'd be livid, says Vivian. Leave the door open.

Fiona stubs out her cigarette on the scaffolding before entering the kitchen. Shame we're mostly stuck at the conference, she says. I haven't visited St. John's since I was a kid. It was great to get out to the gallery, even if the balloon animals were kind of . . . deflating.

I guess that's why none of my friends showed up, says Vivian. Usually openings there are busier. But we mightn't have met otherwise.

The ambient babble from the fridge suddenly seems to intensify, like an orchestra tuning up underwater.

Is that video game music? says Fiona.

Hey, Vivian! Noah calls from the living room. Can I try this thing?

Noah scrambles out from behind the pinball machine as Vivian and Fiona enter the living room. Sorry, he says, I should've asked before plugging it in. I couldn't help myself.

Oh no worries, says Vivian. Scott doesn't let anyone leave the house without trying it.

The pinball machine beckons them in. Rings of tiny lights ripple and radiate. Wire luges loop and zag above a painted backdrop of a man wielding a harpoon gun against a frenzy of cartoon sharks. The marquee on the backbox says *Waterworld*.

Is that supposed to be Kevin Costner? says Fiona.

It's awesome, is what it's supposed to be, says Noah. He pulls and releases the plunger and a metal ball thwacks into orbit. It ricochets wildly through the flashing obstacle course as Noah hammers buttons. The machine clatters and a robotic voice cackles maniacally over a soundtrack of xylophones and machine-gun fire.

Have you ever seen the movie? asks Noah. It's spectacularly bad.

Like cult-classic bad, teases Vivian, or balloon-pufferfish bad? The ball plunks down between the flippers despite Noah's frantic mashing. A red light wails like an ambulance.

Guys, I hate to kill the mood, says Fiona, but this thing is like an amp hooked up to my headache.

Oh of course. Sorry, Fiona. Noah bends down behind the machine and cartoon Kevin Costner sinks into a watery grave. We should get going.

I can walk with you, Vivian says, but I was wondering—would you mind helping me water the plants? Scott has like an entire botanical garden in here. She looks around the living room. Tall potted plants flank the window and the fireplace. Clusters of dark leaves droop down from the tops of bookshelves.

Sure thing, says Noah. Do we need to feed the cat, too?

Scott doesn't have a cat, says Vivian.

Does he have a roommate ... who has a cat?

Nope? It's just Scott.

Well, there's a cat upstairs.

Vivian stands in the doorway of the master bedroom. Noah and Fiona peer over her shoulder at the queen-sized bed, where an armful of orange fur pulses softly on a quilt.

What the ever-loving, says Vivian. Where did you come from?

The cat opens its eyes and yawns. It stares at Vivian for a second, then licks one paw intently and rubs its ears.

Friendly-looking thing, says Noah. Not much more than a kitten. He sits on the bed and the cat rolls towards him and arches its back. It twists its head to look up at him. I guess one of the workers let it in? Noah says. No collar on it.

It could've snuck in through the basement, says Vivian. I should check the windows down there. She sits on the opposite side of the bed and holds out her hand. The cat noses her fingers.

Do you mind if I look around? says Fiona. I love the encaustic at the top of the stairs.

Of course, says Vivian. There's another in the spare bedroom, if it hasn't melted away by now. It gets so hot up here in the summer.

Noah lets the cat nibble his finger. Fi's not much of a cat person, he says. We're dog parents.

Oh, what kind?

A wheaten terrier, says Noah. Her name is Kathy with a K.

Is she very particular about spelling?

It's her full name, "Kathy with a K." Fiona likes to call her Kat to confuse the neighbours.

I'm sure she's very precious.

This one is also very precious, says Noah, rubbing the cat's face. The cat loses interest in his fingers and presses its front paws into Vivian's hip. It kneads and purrs.

I'm a cat person, says Vivian. Who's never owned a cat.

Why not?

My mom is allergic, so I never had one as a kid. And I've just moved a lot. After Dal I lived in Toronto, then I ended up in Oregon for a while, then back to Halifax, then here with my ex.

Oregon?

Portland. Another ex. It's a long story.

But St. John's feels like home?

So far. I mean, this is the longest I've stayed in one place. But Scott's photos always make me think about packing up and travelling for a year or two.

You mean to Ecuador?

Oh, anywhere! Just before I'm too old. I mean, Scott's old but he has a career. That lets him travel like that. I just have a job.

The cat sneezes.

Two drifters meet, says Noah, teasing the cat's ear. Something needs to be exchanged.

What?

Oh, it's from *Waterworld*.

I think it must've gotten in here, Fiona calls from the bedroom at the back of the house. There's a gap under the window frame. From where they're working on the walls.

Really? says Vivian. You think it climbed the scaffolding? She gets up to investigate.

You scamp, says Noah, rubbing the cat's belly. The cat yawns again. Noah yawns too. He scoops up the cat and carries it to the back room.

I'm sure he belongs to the neighbours, says Vivian. Let's leave him in the backyard. He can squeeze under the fence.

She, I think, says Noah. You got a towel or something to plug up that hole in the wall?

It takes twenty minutes to find and water all the plants. Vivian fills Scott's watering can to the brim and hefts it upstairs. Noah fills a tall glass from the sink and hands it up to Fiona, who's brought a chair from the kitchen to reach the pots atop the bookshelves. Then they both fill glasses and tackle the taller plants by the window. There are hanging plants in the kitchen, too. Tiny toy dinosaurs roam among exposed roots.

Vivian waters plants in the bathroom and the bedrooms. There's the spider plant that tickles toilet-sitters. A platoon of succulents on the windowsill in the shower. Spiky things garnishing dressers and bedside tables. She finds a tall plant hiding behind a foldable screen by the window.

Should we do the flowers in the backyard? calls Noah from downstairs.

They should be okay, Vivian says from the spare bedroom. It's supposed to rain. You put the cat out?

She jumped from my arms onto the fence, says Noah. And down into the trees there.

Okay, I'm almost done up here.

Vivian crouches in front of the window. She pulls the bunched-up towel from the gap and feels air flow in from outside. It's less muggy than earlier, and cooler. Scaffolding gleams yellow in the streetlight, and the Buddha ruminates in its corner. The hole in the wall is big enough that Vivian can almost reach out and water the closest maple tree, the moss on the back step. She leaves the towel on the floor. As she smooths out the quilt on the bed she can still hear the spanworms nibbling their nests.

एकत्र Ēkatra

PRAJWALA DIXIT

"Meera?" said a deep, distant voice.

Knuckles hit hard on solid wood. A sharp sound emanated from the bright yellow door of Meera Murti's basement apartment. She traipsed over the once-beautiful oak floors hidden by crumpled pairs of underpants and T-shirts with sweat stains belonging to her cousin, Amy. Jumping over jeans and shoes strewn around an enormous fireplace, she tried to make it as fast as she could to the loud knocking coming from her front door.

"Meera?"

"हो. Yes. One minute!"

Complete with old fireplaces and cedar closets, the apartment was in a sixty-year-old home owned by Jack, a septuagenarian. Its uniqueness was amplified by yellow doors, a characteristic that distinguished it from other homes on the street.

Meera's T-shirt was stained with tears. She wiped her heavy eyes and opened the door. Through the crack, Jack saw Meera use her sleeve to clean her stuffy nose that shone bright in contrast to her pale face. Apart from her cousin, who was working this weekend, Jack was the only human being she knew in this foreign land.

"Is everything all right?"

"Yes . . . no . . . My . . . my . . . hus . . . hus—"

It was the same feeling holding her voice. The one she had felt in seventh standard.

"Do you have my rent today?"

Meera bobbled.

"For fuck's sake! Yes or no?"

"Nnn . . . nnoo."

She watched him stomp away, yelling loud curses into the cold air, to his main-floor apartment where the choicest of profanities landed like big thuds on her ceiling. Closing the door, she felt her feet guide her to the bedroom, where she sank to the floor, wetting it with her tears.

How she wished she could share with someone . . . with anyone . . . the news that had come her way. Her mother-in-law on the phone . . . the inconsolable sobs ringing through the digital airwaves . . . and the phone panning. Meera saw her husband, her Ashwin, inhaling and exhaling with great effort, hooked onto a ventilator in a hospital, desperate for oxygen to fill his virally infected lungs.

She paced the bedroom and tried to call her cousin, Amy, again. The one she had flown across half the world to meet. The beeping ring of the internet call kept pulsing. Amy and her phone were going to be out of Wi-Fi for the next day or so. What was she to do?

She kicked the suitcase over and over again, with all the strength her exhausted self could muster, until it felt like every bone in her body would pierce her skin. For a moment, all she could see were the little lights that dotted her vision. She gathered the clothes she'd put on the floor to pack in a bunch and laid down on them. Feeling her heart move from the speed of light to the rhythmic lub-dub, she closed her eyes.

It was a knock again.

This time on the tiny window of her room, through which the sun had broken in, highlighting the dancing particles in its path, splashing its warmth onto her skin. She felt as if she had stepped on a large turntable that spun round and round. The morning light hit her face, forcing her pupils to dilate. She closed them. The soft darkness comforted her. She didn't even know when it happened, but the loud rap on her window had woken her again. Her eyes moved, focusing to narrow the source of the sound. Another rap. And there it was—a blue jay tapping away at an acorn on her windowsill.

A summer breeze fluttered pieces of paper, fading and fragile as the condition of her husband, who lay miles away fighting for his life, drawing Meera's attention away from the bird. She picked them up from the sun-kissed floor and began reading the elegant penmanship on the wispy pieces of paper, for the umpteenth time.

7th July 1890
Calcutta

Dear Catherine,

I received your letter dated 25th February and am proceeding to answer the same. I set sail yesterday morning. I was to have sailed the previous week. But the Almighty made other plans for me. The weather wasn't on our side. The heavens opened their doors and showered rains delaying my travel. The intention was to start for Canada accompanied by my husband. But he needs to fulfill his responsibilities as a son to his aged mother. Added to this, our pockets extended enough for only one of us. With his encouragement, today I sit at this beautiful desk writing to you amidst the waters of the Bay of Bengal.

I was introduced to the ladies that are accompanying me only after I reached the ship, the Maharajah. Their reception towards me was at best lukewarm. They feel it their duty to press the claims of Christianity and in no way can believe that I intend to remain a devout Hindoo. Yet, none of this matters. I am giddy with delight thinking that the Almighty has set everything aside to focus his energies on me and my dreams. Of studying with women like you. Of thinking of a life as a physician.

Many are contrary to my departure without a man accompanying me in my foreign travels. Many align with the religious ideology that prohibits us from crossing the borders of our Motherland. Such minds are narrow.

I pity their limitations. But let there be no doubt: I am not discouraged. In fact, their opposition strengthens me. The men of my land have forgotten what we Indian women are capable of. Our wisdom, bravery and endurance are overlooked. But these will be badges that I will wear on this journey. Perhaps, it will be a mistake to say this out loud. But I remain glad to embark on this travel by myself outside the shadows of my country and my husband.

The Maharajah will be sailing to Hong Kong. I anticipate disembarking, and will spend the rest of the evening at the accommodations the Missionary has arranged for me. I will write more in the days that pass. For now, I want to immerse myself in the sounds of the water that surround me. In it, I find the Almighty. In it, I see the shakti to carry forward on this path.

Nandini Rao

Meera Murti pressed the big blue button that had "F L U S H" stamped on it. A loud roar rang through the tiny cubicle, making her jump backwards. In the same moment, knuckles hit hard on the opposite side of the bathroom's plastic door, against which she was resting her back. A series of sharp raps hammered on the grey-and-white door and cut through the incessant airplane noise that hummed like one of those thundering air conditioners whose butts stuck out the windows in the gullies of Pune where, under the canopy of old gulmohar and banyan trees, the dabeliwala and butta maushi would compete to sell their food by yelling loud cries that to a foreign ear might signal war.

The only time the two would become one is when the snooty restaurateur, who shared the gully with them, would ask them to move their carts. Meera always felt that there was something brewing . . . some chakkar happening . . . between the dabeliwala and butta maushi. She smiled, thousands of feet up in the air, at the thought of the two of them dancing around trees and lip syncing to "Dil ka bhanwar kare pukar pyaar ka raaz suno, pyaar ka raaz suno re . . . hmm. hmm. hmm."

And there it was again. The knocking. Faster. Fiercer.

"Ma'am, is everything all right?"

"Yes. Yes."

"There are people waiting here . . ."

"Okay. Sorry. Very sorry. Okay. एक . . . one minute . . ."

Meera stood in front of the mirror, her jeans half-down, her headset accessorizing her neck. Between her legs stretched a pair of red cotton underwear, the ones her mother had bought for her, most likely, from the man who sat at the corner of Laxmi Road and Tulsi Baug. She could tell from the multicoloured triangles that patterned the red chaddi. She looked down at the floor and inhaled deeply.

How she wished she was in a second-class train compartment's toilet. The toxic filth was never confined to just the loo in an Indian Railways train and, often, mould would feast on the grimy, brownish growth on what one could assume were once yellow walls. Despite this, Meera missed the second-class train compartment's toilet. For its simplicity. She knew how to work the toilet and the sink. How to clean her backside that now was dotted with goosebumps from the cool air that filled the contraption she was trapped in, flying over the English Channel.

"Ma'am?!"

The same voice spoke again, pretending to stir away its annoyance, adding extra spoonfuls of saccharine.

"We will be landing soon. Could you step out, please?"

"Sorry. Just . . . one minute . . . really sorry."

She had spoken to her cousin, Amy, in detail about this moment. Of using toilet paper. For the very first time in her life. But nothing would ever prepare her for this. Pulling on the roll, she tore the paper. Her eyes closed as her hands felt their way around her behind.

21st July 1890
Hong Kong

Dear Catherine,

I do not feel at home in Hong Kong. Their diet, manners and customs are so varied from ours. When I arrived at the residence that the Missionary had offered for my stay, the neighbours gathered around to have a look at me. Some even peeped through the window. I don't speak their tongue and they didn't speak English. So, we just stared at each other. Occasionally, a child would touch my saree and my skin until their mother pulled their hands off my body. A woman came over and stared at the Nath on my nose and felt the Mangalsutra around my neck. She turned to someone I believe must have been a friend and began conversing in what I suspected must have been rapid Cantonese.

I found myself in their shoes too, my eyes consuming the clothes the women and children wore... the elaborate robes of white and red... and the way they tied their hair in a bun. I could understand our mutual and innocent curiosity. They didn't bother me. It is the expectations of the Missionaries that tires me endlessly. They continue to demand that I deck myself in the finest sarees and best jewels to attend their social gatherings, mostly for upper-class British officers and their wives, where they seek to use me as a token to attract deeper interest in their work. Cautious stares and rude glances are bestowed freely upon me as I am paraded around like the stolen Koh-i-Noor that decks the Crown. It was freeing to walk the streets of

Hong Kong in the cover of the night, where I could hide in the shadows of the dark.

It is of strange nature that makes my mind think to share this memory with you at this moment. Perhaps, because it was in the cover of the night that these events unfolded several years ago. My only child was born in my fourteenth year while my husband and I were living in Pimpri. It lived about ten days and died as there was no competent physician to help us. I do not wish the helplessness that encumbered me in its last minutes to befall anyone. This is what first led me to think of pursuing medicine.

Thousands have been contrary to this desire, violently opposing the education of a woman. But my husband has always expressed a warm interest in female education. It was he who urged me to continue my learning in Bombay. I remain unsure if you remember with clarity, but a few years ago he had published a letter in the Missionary Review that you came across while at your medical studies.

When I think of how we have found your support on this journey, my heart rises with happiness like the water does on a full moon's night. I am eager to see you, to submit to acquiring more knowledge in the field and returning to my country as a Hindoo woman and a doctor.

For now, I must take your leave. We prepare to depart for Yokohama at sunrise. The Empress of India will take me to Vancouver, closer to my dreams and to you.

Nandini Rao

Some were sitting, a few snoring, most walking fast, pulling their trolleyed bags with purpose—Heathrow swarmed with people. Airport carts pushed from one side to another, clinging and clanging, amid the clattering footsteps of harried travellers. The lounge music drowned under the influence of busy eateries packed one next to another, all clamouring to serve the sleep-deprived transit passengers. The duty-free shops were doused in perfume. A swish of air carried the sweet smell and acerbic taste to Meera's nostrils and mouth.

This is what a Benetton ad must feel like, thought Meera, turning round and round, taking in every new face that walked by her. She had never seen so many white people. Ever. Unless she counted her history textbook that was filled with angry-looking British officers dressed in military uniforms, their chins high up in the air.

One of the travellers caught Meera's eye, smiled and said "Hello." And all she did was stare as she walked away, half-smiling. It wasn't the first time she felt almost star-struck by whiteness. In seventh standard, she had seen two tall, white men, one dressed in a red T-shirt and a pair of jeans, his Calvin Klein underwear sticking out, and the other in a dark green kurta and jeans, walk onto the stage during school assembly, right after they had sung "All Things Bright and Beautiful." Mrs. Matthews, in her crisp orange saree, peering over her large glasses, boomed in to the microphone.

"Students. Please welcome Mr. Nathan Field and Mr. Perry Reed."

They waved. First Kurta. And then Calvin Klein.

"They are from National Geographic. And are here to spend time in our school. They will be visiting each section in every standard. I expect nothing but the best from you all while you interact with them."

There was something different in the manner Mrs. Matthews spoke to Kurta and Klein. Her body hunched a little and she seemed to nod at everything they said. And what was with that titter spurting out of her mouth every two seconds? Meera watched the woman who made five hundred children, teachers, and staff shiver every morning with her cold "Good morning" work hard to win the two white men's approval. Like her world would stop if they didn't like her.

"Meera. Come on up here."

Kurta and Klein were in Meera's class, Kurta with a pen and notebook in hand and Klein shouldering a large camera. He smiled and held his hand out, which Meera shook, avoiding any kind of eye contact. Of course, her classmates stifled their laughter but not enough that she couldn't hear it.

"Meera. Tell him about the Damodar Valley Project. What did you learn about it last week?"

Even though she knew she had been pulled up because she spoke the best English in her class, Meera stuttered, taking deep breaths, trying to string together a cohesive sentence.

"It's okay. Take your time."

Kurta's voice was warm, like the smell of freshly made ghee filling her nostrils. As she spoke, loosening up, she became very conscious of her precisely enunciated Indian diction punctuating his free-flowing American accent.

The continuous beeping of an airport buggy pierced her memories. And the growl of the Indian aunty driving it made Meera jump out of her way. She knew one thing very well. India ho ya Heathrow, never get in the way of a disgruntled Indian woman. Stepping aside and straightening her luggage, Meera looked for the nearest foreign-exchange counter.

"How can I help you?"

She smiled at the gentleman in his forties, the few hairs he had neatly parted to the side. He straightened his tie.

"From India?"

Meera nodded.

"हिन्दी आती है?"

"हाँ."

"कहाँ से, इंडिया में?"

"पुणे."

"अच्छा, बॉम्बे के पास . . . First time?"

Meera nodded again.

"डरना नहीं. ये तो रोज़ का हैं. उधर देखो on the left . . . उधर से एस्केलेटर लो और ऊपर जाओ. Best Indian food! और बोलना रूपी अंकल ने भेजा हैं. आपको डिस्काउंट देंगे."

Meera bobbled, handing the money she wanted exchanged. She watched him count the crisp five-hundred-rupee notes. Just before leaving for Canada, Meera had made a trip to her local bank, where an aunty had kept a bundle of ten crisp five-hundred-rupee notes ready, just for Meera. She'd withdrawn almost all she had saved over the two years, teaching maths and English from tuition classes she ran from five to eight every evening. Meera handed the Gandhiji printed notes to Rupee Uncle in Heathrow.

एक, दोन, तीन, चार, पाच . . . . . दहा.

Five thousand rupees.

He placed it into a machine that whirred and swallowed the money, spitting out the Queen's face on purple and green notes.

"लो, इकहत्तर पाउंड्स और ये रहे आपके तैंतालीस पेन्स."

That's it? Five thousand rupees reduced in a moment to less than a hundred pounds?

"Don't worry, beta. आदत पड़ जायेगी."

25th November 1900
St. John's

माझ्या प्रिय गंगाधर,

मला खूप भीती वाटते आहे. इथे सेंट जॉन्स मधे भारताच्या बातम्या मिळत नाहीत| आम्ही द मेल अँड एम्पायरचे सबस्क्रिप्शन घेतले पण भारतात कॉलराचे बातमी जास्ती मिळत नाही. आता तुमच्या आरोग्य कसा आहे? कॉलरा खूप हानिकारक असतो. खूप पाणी प्या. आई, भाऊसाहेब आणि ऋतुजाला पण उकळून पाणी द्यावी. भारतात डॉक्टरांचि कमी आहेस, पण माझे हात बांधलेले आहे.

Please मला पत्र लिहा, मी खूप काळजीत आहे.

सदैव तुमचीच,

नंदू

"आदत पड़ जायेगी, Asian Vegetarian Meal?"
"कशाला ओरडते आहे? मी त्यांना सांगेन! एक मिनीट."
"अरे, मी बोलते आहे आणि तुम्हाला वाटते कि मी ओरडतोय आहे!"
"मीराबाई! हा घ्या! माझा साष्टांग नमस्कार!"

Meera smiled, thinking of the memory of her man, prostrate in defeat in front of her. And then her face filled with heat as she remembered the tender moments that followed.

"Ma'am."

The chashni-se-bhi-sweet voice arrived with a tray.

"We don't have Asian Vegetarian Meals on board."

"No. No. But husband . . . He order. Look . . . here on my ticket."

"Do you eat pork?"

"Poke?"

"Porrrk. Uh . . . pig."

"Cheee! Kai sangthe! No. Vegetarian. Please. Vegetarian. No meat. No eggs. Please."

Air travel was a luxury most of the people in Meera's life couldn't afford. The foreign returns Meera had encountered at a relative's or neighbour's wedding often touted sky-high-cuisine while chomping away on chaat and papdi, the imli chutney dripping over their finery. Envious, she'd wonder if she would ever get a chance to join the mile-high-club, a phrase she had heard at one such gathering where the aunties and uncles were explaining to each other what it meant.

"Aarey. Those points . . . jo card ke saath you get . . . when my Mrs. goes shopping . . ."

"Acha?"

"Haan. Toh woh jab collect ho jata hain . . . then you get to join the mile-high club."

The high-pitched voice of the stick-thin uncle, whose moustache trembled with every word he delivered as he sipped

Chivas Regal, had floated through the air, and fallen on Meera's ears, making her think, with a pinch of pride, that she had made it to this coveted mile-high club too, by earning points and racking up travel miles on her card, like stick-thin Uncle's Mrs. had done.

"Ma'am, all we have on board is a standard vegetarian meal."

Meera opened the plastic coating covering the tray. An earthy smell of bread and greens hit her nose. Her eyes scanned for things familiar. A dal, roti, sabzi. But all she saw was a noodle-like main, with paneer-like cubes sitting on top and some vegetables on the side. She picked up one of the cubes and held it to her nose. A second later, it churned like rubber in her mouth. She had expected the familiar smooth, soft texture of paneer, but instead struggled to gulp the chewy cube of protein. Spitting it out, she decided to stick with the fruits, veggies, and of course the bread.

"Excuse me . . . uh . . . excuse me."

It was a passenger. The first Black man Meera ever spoke with. His eyes sparkled and his lips broadened into a kind smile.

"Is this yours?"

He held a black-and-white photo in his hand.

"It fell when she placed your tray."

"Thank you. Thank you. This very special. Thank you."

Meera gazed at the photograph. Its subject was no older than herself. The bindi that adorned the lady's forehead centred her blunt features. A stunning nath sparkled on her left nostril. The nath, despite being a grand piece of jewellery, seemed dull in contrast to the woman's piercing eyes that oozed fierce pride, making her stand as tall as royalty.

Meera could only imagine the colours of the beautiful saree that the woman had expertly draped. Even in black and white, they had a rich aura, the hand-woven threads creating a fluid piece of cloth that covered the woman's shoulder and flowed down her front. A blouse with puffed sleeves completed the ensemble. The lady wore the saree in an unconventional manner, draping the pallu of her saree over her right shoulder instead of her left.

"How old is that picture?" The Black man handed her the photograph.

"Uh . . . 1892 or 1893 . . ."

"Wow! Who is she?" he asked.

"She very special. She first woman in the family to become a doctor. And first also to settle in Canada."

"Yes?"

"I didn't know she my relation."

"Oh? How is she related to you?"

"माझ्या आजीच्या आईची ताई." Meera replied. "Uh . . . my grand-mother's mother . . . great grandmother's sister."

"Hey! Now that you mention it . . . I see the resemblance . . . you have her beautiful eyes."

Meera smiled. Was he flirting? Should she tell him she was married?

"Where did she live in Canada?"

"First Vancouver. And then New-found-land. St. John's."

"She's seen the country. Coast to coast!"

"She married white man."

"Really? Back then?"

"Yes. Very धाडसी . . . uhh . . . bold . . . guts . . . gutsy woman."

"What was her name?"

"Nandini . . . Nandini Rao."

6th October 1902
St. John's
India Office Records
Dominion of India

Sir,

Herewith are the names of my family members in India. They are not in direct employment of the British Raj. However, I have been working with a British Missionary that now places me in service of the people of Newfoundland. Please inform me in regards to their deaths, if recorded in your registry.

For the foreseeable future, the Missionary has dictated that I continue to work for them, in St. John's, the assigned post, to repay them for the educational opportunities they provided. I remain desperate for any news in relation to my family. The last I was intimated about them was two years ago, on the 15th of June 1900, from Pune, when they informed me of the outbreak of cholera in India due to which my husband and two sisters had fallen ill.

Please do the needful.

Nandini Rao

<u>Names of my family members</u>
1. Sumitra Rao, 60 years (w/o late Kelkar Rao, my mother-in-law)

2. Gangadhar Rao, 37 years (s/o Sumitra Rao and late Kelkar Rao, my husband)

3. Makrand Rao, 34 years (s/o Sumitra Rao and late Kelkar Rao, my brother-in-law)

4. Rutuja Rao, 22 years (w/o Makrand Rao, my sister-in-law)

5. Shalini Deshmukh, 28 years (w/o Vilas Deshmukh, my sister)

6. Shwetha Deshpande, 25 years (d/o late Poorva Deshpande and late Uddhav Deshpande, my sister)

<u>Last known address</u>

Maruti Chowk
Shukrawar Peth
Pune

(Personal Copy)

18th January 1912
St. John's

Gangadhar,

मला माहिती नाही की तुम्हाला हे पत्र मिलेळ कि नाही, मी रोज तुमचा विचार करते आणि तुझ्या आरोग्य साठी बाप्पाला प्रार्थना करते.

I feel desolate . . . orphaned . . . not having heard from any of you in these ten years. Even though my heart wants to believe that you are still alive and well, my soul doesn't feel your presence any more on this earth. In these ten years, a lot has changed. I met someone. His name is Patrick.

मला माहिती आहे कि you would want me to move on in life. माझ्या आनंदमयी जीवनासाठी तुम्ही महत्व दिले, and keeping this in mind, I am starting a new chapter in life. But before I do so, I wanted to check one last time to see if I would hear a response back to this letter जर तुमाला हे अवडत नसेल, तर मला कृपया सांगा, हा माझी नवीन पत्ता आहे.

मी नेहमी च . . . always . . . always love you.

या जीवनात and in the seven more to come.

तुमची,

Nandu

A quilt of chirps and tweets flowed in through the window with the flood of light. Meera sat still. The pieces of paper, browned on the edges and filled with the fading ink of Nandini's words, hung limp in her hand. The unsteady vibrations of her phone reminded her of the pain the letters echoed through the words they carried. She saw the bluish hue emerge from the pile of clothes before rummaging for the phone. A moment later, her mother-in-law's face popped up on the screen.

"मीरा . . . अगह मीरा . . . अश्विन . . . अश्विन तुझा नाव घेत आहे. तुला भेटायचे आहे अंस—

"आई—"

"मी काय सांगू त्याला—"

"आई!!"

The birds twittered a happy tune outside the window. Meera stood up and began to gather her belongings, the ones on the floor and those that were in a neat pile inside the top two drawers of a dresser Amy had cleaned out for her.

"मी घरी येते."

"मी सांगितले . . . तुला आणि अश्विनला . . . एकत्र जायला . . . मी सांगित—"

"आई—"

Meera threw the clothes with force into the opened suitcase, annoyed by her mother-in-law's fifteenth reminder that she had told the couple to travel together.

"तू कशाला नाराज होते आहे?"

'मी व्यवस्था करूं घरि पाऊचें, चिंता नक्को करा, आता फोन अश्विन ला द्या."

Tears streaked her face as her mother-in-law turned the phone towards her husband.

"काय रे? तू माझ्या शिवाय सात दिवस पण जगु शकत नाही का?"

Meera watched a small smile light up Ashwin's face as his eyes closed and head moved ever so slightly from side to side.

"मी येते, तू कुठेच जाऊ नको."

As she waved and blew him a kiss, her mother-in-law's face loomed back into focus.

"मी जाऊन तैयारी करते आणि तुम्हांला नंतर फोन करता. Okay. Okay. Bye."

"Bye. Bye. Bye—"

"Bye."

The St. John's International Airport she had arrived in and the one she now found herself departing from felt as different to look at as her and her nearly white cousin, Amy. An emptiness covered every inch of the space, snug like a fitted sheet on a mattress. Travellers and their Tim Hortons coffee were apocalyptically absent.

The sounds of creaking wheels and footsteps reverberated through the vacant airport, broken only by the occasional announcement sputtering through the sound system announcing the new travel restrictions due to the pandemic.

Meera and Amy stopped at the baggage counter. The whir of the sanitizer pump was followed by a woman dressed in a navy-blue suit, her hair tied into a sleek ponytail, rubbing every crevice of her hands.

Amy tilted her head towards Meera.

"Are you sure? Tu sure aahes ka?"

"हो. Me sure."

"I know he needs you. But . . . Pan . . . Khup risky . . . to travel . . . aata. How about you wait for a few more weeks?"

"I go. त्याला माझी गरज अहे . . . umm . . . he need me. Most."

"Hi there!" the woman in navy had interjected through the blue mask that covered all her face except the hazel eyes that looked from Meera to Amy with a polite curiosity.

"Hi! This is my cousin. She's travelling to India."

"Passport, please."

Once Meera had got off the phone with her mother-in-law, she knew she had to track down Amy. Even if she felt afraid to speak English with foreigners, she knew she couldn't sit waiting while Yama crept closer to her husband. Her heart fluttered away as she marched up the stairs to Jack's apartment, preparing to be yelled at for her poor communication skills. How she wished Jack knew how intelligent she sounded in Marathi.

There was knocking again. And for a change, it was her knuckles hitting the solid wood of Jack's yellow door.

"Hello, sir. Sorry I disturb."

"Yes?"

"My cousin . . . Amy . . . her phone off."

"Okay."

"I need . . . uhh . . . talk her."

"Speak with her?"

"Yes. Yes! She told to me . . . Meera I work emergency. So my phone off."

"Oh?"

"You know hospital number? My husband very sick . . . with corona. In India. Help please?"

Jack turned out to be a bhalla manus. His frustration from the previous night stemmed from the fact that Amy was always late with her rent, either overworked or overtired because of the endless shifts she picked up as an ER doctor. But geniality and humanity, which had been stitched into his Newfoundland heart by his beloved Nan, overtook him when he saw Meera on his doorstep. Always be a good Christian, Jack, his Nan had said to him since he wasn't taller than the rubber boots that hung in her shed. He dialled every number related to the hospital services until they had tracked down Amy.

"I still can't believe you got Jack to warm up to you! He's such a curmudgeon."

"काय ?" Curzon?"

"No. Curmudgeon. Uhh . . . khadoos!"

The women's laughter filled the air, dancing a tune with the light that filtered through the large windows.

"Listen. Sit. Ithe basa."

Meera sat next to Amy who held her hand, their brown and white skins intertwined in a tight lock.

"I am so, so, so glad you travelled this far, just to meet me. After I lost my parents, I never thought that I would have anyone to call family again. But look. The universe brought us together."

It had begun with a Google search with the names and the address provided in the letters Nandini had received and written. Facebook and Instagram also narrowed down the search. One morning, a random message popped on Meera's phone that said, "Hi. My name is Amy Rao McKim. This will sound very weird. But I think we're related."

"त्यांची uhh . . . energy . . . spirit . . . आम्हाला एकत्र आणते . . ."

"Ēkatra?"

Meera lifted their joined hands up, indicating what she was trying to say.

"Strange how it all happened, right? I found all of those letters, the names . . . her photograph . . . while cleaning out my mother's things from their old home . . . one thing led to another . . ."

"देवाची इच्छा . . . नंदिनी माऊशीची इच्छा."

"I'm guessing she would be happy today . . ."

"Not would be . . . she be . . . she is happy. मला माहिती आहे."

Meera's eyes welled up as she watched Amy place a kiss on their locked hands. They held each other in a tight embrace, exuding a warmth that even freshly baked cookies couldn't match. When they broke apart, they continued to hold each other by their arms, staring into each other's eyes. Meera wiped Amy's tears and planted a kiss on her cousin's cheek. They held hands again walking towards security, where big boards were placed highlighting the proper use of masks. Neither said anything, as they were interrupted by an airport announcement.

"Please respect the two-metre distance to queue at areas in the airport terminal building. The safety of our passengers, employees and our community is our top priority. Thank you."

It was a strange bond of genetics, of brownness, of culture, of family, forged on an island in the middle of the North Atlantic.

"Next time . . . तुझी पाळी."

"What?"

"Your turn . . . to come India. Meet family. Your family. आणि प्रक्टिस तुझी मराठी. विसरु नाका?"

"I promise we'll speak in shuddh Marathi jheva I visit Pune. Bara?"

"नक्की?"

"Aai shapath!"

the years the locusts have eaten

BRIDGET CANNING

I remember the smell of burnt dirt and hot metal. We thought the bombs would do in the Germans. We thought it would break their legs from under them. But their shots sang to us as we went over the top. Nigel, the messenger boy, was on the right and Belemy on my left when I saw the boy go down. I said, The boy is gone, Belemy. And I looked left and Belemy wasn't there.

The tourism association wants me to headline a "commemorative performance" on July 1st. It'll be a regular feature in the local news, a prompt to plump up Newfoundland history for the summer crowd. So far, I've refused. But I'm just being contrary. For every go, there has to be a last time and this is my fourth. When it's over, so am I.

It doesn't take much to vanish when you know what you're doing. If it wasn't already done to death, I could write a song about ways to slip away:

Step one, make vices visible. Leave bottles onstage. Trip on them. Flirt with inappropriate people. Mouth off. Later, they will say how sad it was to see me so consumed.

Step two, play out a few scenes. For last Friday's gig, I made sure I was two hours late. Last month, I showed up without the band. Both times, I shrugged off the bar's frustration and drank bourbon. Heads shook and phones flashed. Disappointment moves fast these days.

Step three, pretend to age. For every go, create an image. When the time is right, add age's influence. Dark glasses into bifocals, red spats into orthopedic shoes. Adopting a trend and wearing it out also works. A ripped bowler hat. Greasy bell-bottoms.

When it's close to disappearing time, I let the one hundred lost boys show on my face. They're always just behind my eyelids. Although nowadays they blur into fresher betrayals. Like the face of the backup singer in New York City, 1982, the dreams in her dark eyes full and bright as I passed her the needle.

Or Sarah, her voice full of tears, "You can make him into a song, but you can't be there for me." Or the way all three waved goodbye as they boarded that crappy little plane. Once I let them show, I'm basically done. Everybody knows someone who got old all of a sudden.

This summer makes it a century that I've been running this gig. A hundred years of songs about war and loss. Now called upon to sing on the anniversary of my utmost betrayal. Damn you, Littlefair. You love your irony.

Maudsley was the biggest moaner at Grimsby. The war will be done before the lot of us are trained, he said. The Fifth Lincolns are already up to standard. We don't even have uniforms yet. Would be just my luck to finally get my hands on a rifle and the action dries up.

Action. There was daily talk of it. How great it must be, how unfair if we don't get any, how hard it will be to tolerate those who get some.

Maudsley believes action will get him everything he wants.

The ladies prefer heroes, he says. Walk into a dance with medals on your chest? You can take your pick.

I grinned and cheered with the rest. I didn't dare speak the secrets of my guts. Or admit the action I truly desired was time, opportunity, and process.

Lord Kitchener ensured we had no choice. Lady Doughty named us The Chums. We're all chums, every bloomin' one of us! A quarter million underage volunteers. If Kitchener lived today, he'd be accused of propaganda or romanticizing violence. Or at least peer pressure. His signs hung on every public wall:

> WAKE UP GRIMSBY!
> YOUNG MEN, DO YOUR DUTY.
> JOIN NOW WITH YOUR PALS.
> YOUNG WOMEN, ENCOURAGE THE MEN
> TO DO THEIR DUTY.
> 500 MEN FROM ALL CLASSES
> MUST BE RECRUITED AT ONCE.
> DON'T IMAGINE YOU ARE NOT WANTED.
> YOUR COUNTRY NEEDS YOU.
> MEN CAN ENLIST IN THE NEW ARMY
> FOR THE DURATION OF THE WAR.
> VOLUNTEERS FOR SERVICE ABROAD URGENTLY
> WANTED FOR THIS REGIMENT.

Not that I considered the alternative. Choices were filmy daydreams I'd get caught drifting in. Ol' Fletcher, off in the clouds. I descended into woolgathering as I watched a band or passed the music store and its window of gleaming instruments. My fingers ached to understand them. My belly burst with hot envy when I was confronted with those who could create musical magic, who knew more than a few party pieces to make their family dance at Christmas.

And my daydream clouds never dispersed, not even during basic training. Which was all a spot of sport. Gathering at the Brocklesby Cricket Club to dig trenches. Eagerly stabbing sandbags with bayonets. I played along and craved my comrades' other talents: Tommy Ellis's rich tenor voice made everyone's eyes shine when he sang "God Save the Queen." Frank Tefford's easy manner with lyrics and rhymes, his clever poems about the retired NCOs who trained us. Ernst Belemy and his fiddle. Even Maudsley's great whistle, piping along on his journey to become the heroic soldier who eventually gets laid.

Every start flowed like a new river. I arrived in a city, I earned enough busking to afford a room, enough saloon-playing to pay for meals. I attracted friends. They offered couches, spare beds. Women warmed to me. I got gigs collaborating with local musicians. I went on tours. I met more important friends. The music flexed within me, spreading open like a paper fan.

But the songs remained the same. A mining accident in a coal-industry town. A factory burns down. A woman escapes a violent man. Refugees sink to the bottom of the sea. I collected a hundred dreary nicknames: The Voice of the Voiceless, The Unveiler, Troubadour of Tragedy. Legends emerged on how I simply "appeared" one day. The bastard son of Johnny Cash and Peggy Lee. Reincarnation of Woody Guthrie. Sold my soul at a crossroads for talent. I don't like that one.

When I noticed him crouched beside me, I thought, why is he still in blue serge? We were issued khakis long ago. But the crater was dark and his clothes could have been black or blue.

Who are you? I said.
Littlefair, he answered. You?
Fletcher. Norman Fletcher.
You're in a tight spot, Norman.

I hadn't heard my first name on another's lips since we left England. It felt foreign and soothing, like Littlefair himself. When he spoke, there was a lilt and shifting in his dialect, like it was dodging recognition. He was a little everything, British, French, perhaps even German. And calm. I believed he was a hallucination. It seemed natural he was a result of my brain, scrabbling to escape this disaster.

Poor ol' Maudsley, Littlefair said. All he wanted was a chance to get into Betty Titter's skirts. The dream really got to him.

What dream? I wanted him to say this is the dream, this is all a dream.

His dream of being a certain kind of man. He lit a cigarette and passed it to me. What kind of man did you dream of being?

It doesn't matter now, I said. If it's a living man, I'll be lucky.

Oh, Norman. Of course it matters.

A sharp cry from up ahead. Someone's muffled orders. No, it really doesn't, I said.

Ever tell anyone your dreams?

God, no.

Why not?

We're in a war. Dreams are foolish.

You think the Germans don't have dreams?

Yeah, and look where it's gotten us. I mopped sweat off my face. A groan from somewhere behind me. Just a matter of time and shrapnel.

I think you should get them off your chest.

Littlefair shifted closer. His voice floated into my ear. We all have them, he said. Maudsley, Belemy. Why not take some time for yourself before it's too late? Like the Catholics do with confession.

It works for them, doesn't it? I said.

Oh yes. Everyone needs solace sometimes.

I only wanted music. My eyes got hot. What if I started weeping, right there? Blind with tears and shot in the guts. Sobbing over a pipe dream.

In what way?

Make it and be it. Be a musician.

That sounds lovely.

It's pathetic.

Why? You don't think it's a worthy desire?

It's a dream of pride.

At this, he gestured around, the smouldering, quaking hole: This isn't a dream of pride?

This is war. And bloody fucking duty, I said. I wiped my eyes. Okay. Done with it. Keep quiet about dreams.

Littlefair laughed, a tinny, musical sound. Oh, Norman. We both know this war is the most prideful dream of all.

I shifted away from him. His silvern laugh and fresh grave eyes made me queasy. Maybe I was dying. Maybe he was my mind, unravelling.

Do you know, Norman, Littlefair said, what the priest will say, next week, when the bodies are finally recovered, when scraps of the living stand at attention by ranks of corpses? I will restore to you the years that the locusts have eaten. That's what he'll say. What do you think it means?

From the Bible.

Bien sûr. It's from the book of Joel. God sent the locusts to destroy Israel's crops. And they were ruined for years. They wiped out all the seed, that year's, the previous years'. All those grape vines and fruit trees, all the possible abundance and life and pleasure, gone. And God states that repentant people will be blessed and restored in heaven. These are the words the priest will offer for solace. And it is what the Lincolnshire families will be left with, on that day, when every young man they know is dead.

Why are you telling me this? How is your guesswork supposed to help me?

Is it guesswork?

How else would you know what a priest will say next week?

I think you know how I know, Norman.

And it was there, in his face. Something reptilian and ancient. Like watching a snake open its jaws.

I looked away, to my right. Maudsley crouched with his hands clasped

in prayer, lips murmuring the litany.
He knows now, Littlefair said, that he was mistaken.
Our father, who art in heaven, Maudsley said. I turned away from him. I looked into the teeth of Littlefair's gaze.

I remember an image often repeated in the early cartoons. There would be a character like Donald Duck, confronted with temptation. Angel and devil versions of himself would appear, one on each shoulder, to whisper options into his ears.

In my experience, the devil on the left doesn't offer new ideas. He simply says it's okay to do what you want. Take the money. Lie to the woman. Pull the trigger.

All Littlefair did was reveal the path and permit indulgence: they're all going to die anyway. Same result in the end.

And there was the path, up and over the pit. I went. My legs churned like watch-wheels. Bullets, blood, and debris slid in a radius around me. I moved past German faces. I could reach out and touch them. If I had a weapon. But that wasn't the deal. I kept on and was unseen. The sounds shrank behind my spine. I realized I was whistling. It was pure and rich, a good whistle. It was Maudsley's whistle. Mine now.

I followed a rail line to the sea, to a farmhouse lit by lamplight. There was an elderly woman, a bed in the back, a violin. We spoke in broken words. The instrument came to life in my hands. I did some repairs around the property. I played her into peace every night.

One night, there was a boat. I floated across to America, into cities and towns, into a rhythm of steady bits of money. I knew how to make people listen, dance, cry, rise up. It was me and not me. When my inheritance surfaced, like Tommy Ellis's voice on the right chord or Frank Tefford's words marching from my pen, I looked for a drink. Or a smoke. Or whatever was handy.

My military haircut grew out curly. I liked looking different. I formulated how to avoid war and duty. Create an obvious handicap, an eye patch, a slight limp, a lean-in-to-hear-better motion. I received first pity, then praise for my songs about heroes. How kind of me to inspire those with a job to do.

I tried a family once. In Nashville, there was Sarah. She taught folk dance and moved with liquid grace.

I have a son, she said. He's ten. Never knew his dad.

I found myself in a quieter place than usual. I played smaller gigs and avoided the glory of spots like Exit/In. For Sarah, I was Clancy Robbins, a poet and folksinger. I believed it would be good for me. I'd make sure her son was free to try and learn and explore. I would never tell him what kind of man to be.

But James was such a boy, a running, jumping, sunburned, laughing little boy. He lived for the outdoors and his friends, and I let them all be free in our home. I taught Stephan, our neighbour, how to play the harmonica, and the music of his practice reached my ears every night. I caught James's best friend, Travis, stealing my guitar picks, his face flushing red to match his ginger hair. I told him he only had to ask.

At eighteen, all they wanted was work and status symbols: trucks, cars, motorcycles. They formed a roofing team, hard work for quick money. Do you really have no more ambition than this? I said. Find something shiny and go as fast as possible? They shrugged. I shrugged in return.

And three weeks later, their employer attended an all-night bachelor party. He thought he'd be in fine shape to drive them to site the next day. Or I imagine that's what he'd say if he or any of them had survived the collision.

If you'd given James a drop of structure, he would have been a man who questioned what he was asked to do, Sarah said. She screamed at my back as I entered my music room. "A Song for

James" bled fast from my fingers. Then it was time to leave. The eighties in New York City provided many ways to forget.

Lately, I've been expecting to see Littlefair. He's appeared three times over the years. I look out into the audience and there he is, grinning and swaying with insincere enthusiasm. Each time, our evenings are infuriatingly soothing. What's better in the long run? he said in Haight-Ashbury. He wore a loud shirt with a flared Capri collar and some kind of plaid pants in surreal blues and yellows. His outfits were always in-jokes, costumed aggregations of the time and place I'm in.

If they'd all survived, how many would be good men? They'd return home shell-shocked. Hit the bottle, hit their wives. They'd raise confused, angry children. Isn't it better, overall, to have contributed to the canon of meaningful art? To make something to help and inspire others? He poured shots until all I saw was the glint of his teeth in the tavern lights. *If you're worried about goodness, dear Norman, all that stuff weighs itself out at the end.*

On July 1st, the Beaumont-Hamel Memorial Concert set-up is predictable: beer tent staggering steps from stage, long stretch of grass littered with takeout containers and stoned bodies. I will not miss any of this. There are ten songs in the set. I'm throwing it in at number four.

I make a point of cursing between songs two and three: How many of you thought this was for fucking Canada Day? Laughter. A *fuck you*. Littlefair dances in the midst of the crowd before the stage, shaking his rump. He wears what looks like a veteran's uniform.

I decide to forget the lyrics of the second verse. I pause and start again. The band scrambles to catch up. The audience grumbles.

Don't act like you never forget things, I say. I sing off-key. I slacken my strumming hand. There's the first boo. Here it comes.

Every time a person boos, an angel gets a venereal disease, I say.

Go home.

Have another drink, b'y.

Maybe I should call them Newfies. Get things hot and bothered. I step forward and let the edge of the guitar smack the microphone stand.

The audience makes faces and exclamations of fear. This was supposed to mean something. They want me to give them something to feel. Not one hundred years of ego and addiction. Suddenly, a personal realization: no one has ever been an addict more than me.

I let the microphone whine too long and I stare at a girl in the front too long and if I do it long enough, Littlefair will let it open and consume me. Like a mouth on a spoon. Like bodies in a pit.

The hands on my waist are strong. Here we go, the voice says. It is the backup guitarist with the ginger beard. He sings my words into the microphone and his voice is velvet luxury. The audience cheers. The band clicks into harmony and it's rescued, the song, the atmosphere, the night. Littlefair holds a lighter high in the air. I let myself hang off the hero guitarist's arm. Look at me, the ruined man.

It's okay, Clancy, the guitarist says. His eyes meet mine. They have freckled eyelids and when he blinks, he is young Travis. The beard is new with his modern look, but it is him, looking as he did the day he hopped in next to James, waved goodbye and was driven into oblivion. You did good, Clancy, he says. It's all good. You can still be done.

Littlefair claps and whoops. In the audience, I see them intermingled amongst the high and drunk, the messenger boy, Maudsley, Tommy Ellis, Erst Belemy. They stand at attention with the patience of disciplined soldiers. They wait for me to take a bow.

what kind of dog is he?

TERRY DOYLE

I lost my dog, Sturdy, in May of last year after he looked directly at the eclipse. Something happened to him. I can't explain it. But if I had to try, I'd probably start with his breath. It changed that day, turned sour and rank. Death is what it smelled like. On hot days his panting could foul any car ride, so I had to leave him home. Before, Sturdy was the recipient of all my kisses. He'd sit, pin his ears flat and raise his nose, holding still while I forced my kisses up and down his furry snout, his little nub of a tail brushing the floor. Who's a good boy? But once he looked at the eclipse and his breath turned ghastly, well, I didn't get that close to his mouth no more. I stopped kissing him. And when he'd lay his chin on my knee and give me that hangdog look, instead of rubbing his ears and scratching around his eyes, like I used to, I started moving my knee and telling him to go away, he stank.

But that wasn't all that changed. After the eclipse, when we hiked the trails, he didn't look back. Before, once I unclicked his leash and said Go on, and he ran ahead to sniff and explore, he would always look back, checking over his shoulder, making sure I was still with him. Not anymore though. He wandered. I spent the better part of two separate afternoons whistling and hollering, trying to get him back after he'd wandered away. It got so I couldn't let him off leash anymore. But he tugged, and if I was forever having to correct his leash manners it sort of defeated the purpose of the walk, which was to let my mind wander. He'd been the excuse that got me outside, walking. Now he was an excuse not to go.

A word that came to me often, whether in the shower, or before falling asleep, or first thing upon waking, was disloyal. I think I could have handled disobedience, or stupidity. But a dog that's not loyal? Why even have a dog? Do you know how, if you're the kind of person who's been lonely, if you've been rejected by those expected to love you, if you spent years crafting psychological walls for protection, do you know how it feels to have your dog stop adoring you? My best friend? Looked at an eclipse and now won't look at me? What could I do?

I took him to the vet. They said he was fine. And I was out three hundred bucks. I took him to a different vet. They wanted to run a series of blood tests and x-rays, the lady in a lab coat practically salivating at the vagueness of symptoms I was describing. Dismayed, I muttered something about Sturdy needing to see a shrink, and she goes, "We have one!"

Shit, I almost went for it too. I wanted him back so bad. Foul breath and everything.

I started watching other dogs. On the street, at the park, each moment of eye contact between them and their masters filled me with envy and a sense that I'd failed at something undefinable.

These other dogs, they had manners, they knew how to fetch, they still loved the way they were meant to. For the briefest moment I blamed myself—for what, I couldn't say, but there was a sense I'd been neglectful. Neglectful of what, I didn't know. Sturdy was well fed, groomed, and housed. He got daily exercise. Which, when I went down through it, meant it couldn't be me. Could it? I was doing my part. I was fulfilling my side of the arrangement. The problem, plainly, was the moon. I didn't understand it—why the moon had it out for me, or how the moon could turn my dog against me—but it was the only explanation available. He looked directly at the eclipse—I seen him—and he changed.

At work there were questions. What was up with me? Problems at home? But what could I say? Tell them how when I got home at six o'clock there was no more excitement at my arrival? How Sturdy didn't so much as lift an eyebrow when I came through the door? I'd sound like a lunatic, wouldn't I? So I said I was depressed. Seasonally depressed. My boss sent me an email with a link for a SAD lamp, noting that our health benefits covered eighty per cent.

Maybe I could leave it on for Sturdy all day. Maybe *he* was depressed. Fuckin jerk.

Anyway, it wasn't long before I devised a plan. I figured I'd say I was taking a vacation or going out of town on business, and I'd ask someone to watch Sturdy while I was gone. Maybe he'd act different. Maybe he'd be his old self without me around—start acting like a normal dog. Or, shit, who knows, maybe he'd miss me.

But who could I ask?

I created a list of candidates. It was a short list, and it took longer to think of the three names on there than it did to think of reasons why I couldn't ask them for help.

There were kennels, doggy daycares, I could try that. But, I thought, at an institution like that he'd just be another dog. They wouldn't be paying him the kind of attention I required. He'd just be a furry face in a crowd—a concept I loathed.

I was lost.

I just wanted him back so bad. I needed to feel again the way he loved me. Even if it was only because I was the one who fed him and walked him. His reasons why weren't important; the feelings it gave me—feeling needed, feeling wanted, even appreciated—they were real, and their absence was tearing me apart.

I took him to the dog park. I thought maybe he *is* depressed. You can always find young, high-energy dogs and their old, low-energy masters at the dog park. I'd see how Sturdy responded. If he mopes, I thought, something's up. With him, not me. If he hates himself, I can handle that. I can relate. But if it's me he hates, now, since the eclipse. Then I don't know. Get in line, I guess.

When we arrived, the park was empty. We went in, I removed his leash and then watched as he sniffed the fenceline with a slack tail. A dirty tennis ball had been discarded, or forgotten, or deemed, suddenly, no good anymore, and lay beside the mud-encrusted bench. Please, I thought as I bent to pick it up, let this ball squeak. I knew any whistle emerging from my unwanted lips was fated to be ignored. I gave the ball a squeeze and saw why it'd been left behind. Its side was split. I tried a whistle anyway. Maybe he was going deaf? Surely that could account for the change in him? But the vet had checked his ears. I watched. Twice. And just before I cocked my arm to throw the rotten ball right at my rotten dog, the squeak of the gate opening raised Sturdy's head and I lowered my fist, which held the ball.

A terrible confusion of feelings raced through me as he raised his nubby tail and stepped lightly toward the newcomer—a mix of joy, at seeing him roused, the knowledge that he wasn't sick, and the horror of a simultaneous realization that it was now, irrefutably, me. I was the problem. Even my dog couldn't bring himself to love me.

But hang on now. There was a raising of hackles, a low, gravelly warning, and then a flashing of teeth. Hope!

Fuck him up, Sturdy, I thought, for some reason. But the lady holding the new dog's leash—clipped to the dog's back, onto a harness, basically instructing the dog to pull and lunge and pursue, tapping into its sled-dog instinct—she didn't like the look of Sturdy. "He's fine," I heard myself say, and would later remember with confusion. But no, she wasn't taking any chances. She backed through the gate, dragging the harnessed dog away against its wishes. I thought about trying to put Sturdy in a harness like that and the contempt with which he would stare at me while I did it. The gate closed, the new dog was gone, and Sturdy turned his back to me and lay down in the dirt.

At home later, trying to conjure another test, one more scenario that could more definitively identify the problem—hopefully pointing away from me—I thought about the dogs of my past. Lucky, my parents' lab mix, who slept, sometimes, on my bed with me, and who once alerted us to a burst pipe in the basement, saving boxes of family photographs, preserving memories painful and sweet. And Soldier, my father's dog after the divorce. An affectionate and protective shepherd whose hips gave out early and who became a burden to my father, until he surrendered her to a shelter, secretly, in the middle of the night. And Missy, my uncle's Great Dane who was so large she went through life with a spotlight on her, like a prisoner trying to escape. She commanded attention, unwillingly, and at just four years old—twenty-eight in dog years—developed what the vet called a cognitive disability, which, he said, accounted for the bouts of incontinence and lack of coordination. My uncle put her to sleep. I thought, very briefly, perhaps I should do the same. But I knew I could not. Then I recalled the cat we'd had when I was very young, and the explanation of its disappearance that's become foggy over time: how my old man, once the cat started spraying the already clawed furniture, took the cat down the shore and heaved it over a cliff, into a gulch. And then, a week later, the cat, just like in the song, came back.

If you love something, let it go, right?

I put Sturdy in the truck and we drove for forty minutes, away from the city, into an area bordering the wildlife preserve where a ghostly herd of caribou allegedly still roamed. I pulled off onto a woods road, branches scraping the truck doors, the ground in turns soft and wet and rocky. I stopped, opened both doors as wide as I could and walked a short distance inland. Sturdy hopped down and followed me. Then I turned back and sat again in the driver's seat. "You got ten minutes," I said, and stuck the key in the ignition.

Ten minutes is a long time. Sitting there, full of anticipation and dread, I fantasized about a new dog. A puppy maybe. Another chance to get it right. Really make something love me. But it was just escapism, just my way of diverting focus from what was present: whether or not Sturdy would come back to me.

Thick, dark clouds started moving in. I could see the rain in the distance. Three minutes had passed. Looking up at the clouds, as the shadow they cast moved slowly forward, I wondered what it was Sturdy saw that day, when he looked at the eclipse. What part of me was revealed to him in that shade? If he could talk, would he be able to articulate it? And if so, would I listen, trying to understand?

There was a sound I thought was distant thunder, but it continued, long, and drawn-out. A growl, like gravel sliding out the back of a dump truck. I stepped out, pushing the door against the branches of alders. Only six minutes had passed. Sturdy was behind the truck, and he was not alone. There was another dog. A beagle. Its eyes were red, its tongue lolled, and the legs on it looked ready to give way. Sturdy was growling, but he stopped when I approached. He looked at me, at my expression, and then he moved behind me. The beagle sat and stared, never breaking eye contact with me, its big, tired eyes pleading—the want in them was palpable. The need. I thought, This is pathetic. Clearly someone had brought this dog out here. Probably they were hunting, but maybe not. This dog, either way, had been left behind. And it repulsed me. The weakness. The need.

"I got nothing for you," I said. The beagle titled its head as if it didn't understand. Then it scratched and dug into its ear, and while it was busy doing that, and had finally taken its eyes off mine, I turned and got back into the truck. I didn't have to call Sturdy. The passenger side door was still open, he hopped up and I reached across him to close it. I pulled on my seatbelt and looked again at the dark clouds. They were here now, raindrops began drumming the roof. I turned the ignition, put the wipers on and put the truck in gear. I looked at Sturdy and this time he looked back at me, his two brown eyes like big, glassy mirrors, and I said, "That could be you. Smarten up."

remains of conception

CARMELLA GRAY-COSGROVE

At the playgroup, my baby is too young to enjoy storytime or playing with blocks, but I go anyway because I need to talk to other adults. Some of the other adults have two kids. A toddler and a younger baby. Not as young as my baby, but young. They carry them in their baby carriers and they recommend that I join the baby-wearing group on Facebook. I have a no-name brand baby carrier that I bought off Marketplace. I struggle to strap it on to myself—it's designed for a second person to clip it together across the shoulder blades, but if I twist I can do it, with a little strain on my right rotator cuff, which is getting very flexible. The flexible rotator cuff is just one of several imbalances I've developed since having the baby. The others are a strong left bicep from carrying the baby with my left arm so I can do things with my right, and a larger left breast, which the public health nurse says is totally normal and means I have more milk ducts on that side.

The public health nurse visited me at home the month after I gave birth to make sure I was not developing postpartum depression. She called it the baby blues. The public health nurse had streaked blond hair which she touched a lot and I thought about how it was unhygienic. She did that thing where she would comb her fingers through the front of her hair and swoop it to the side. I could hear her nails scraping against her scalp. The public health nurse said she herself had one breast that produced more milk when she breastfed her own babies. She said she nicknamed her breasts the stud and the dud. She said the baby had a beautiful round head.

"Hashtag goals," said the public health nurse.

I told her it was so round because he wouldn't let me put him down.

The public health nurse asked what my neighbours are like. I told her there was just one old woman in the building, in the downstairs apartment. I did not say that I thought I felt something in the apartment with me, a tiny heaviness when I stopped moving. Or that I could feel it between us at that very moment. She made a note in my file, presumably about the neighbour, but maybe it was unrelated.

When the public health nurse weighed the baby, she said he was in the ninety-seventh percentile for weight.

"Mama's making milkshakes," she said.

A few years before this baby I was pregnant with another baby but very early on I started bleeding and the baby didn't end up turning into a baby. I called my gynecologist and he said he could suck it out to speed things up and I said okay. He had been awake for twenty-four hours delivering babies, but he came in anyways, after hours. When I got to the clinic near the Health Sciences

Centre, he did an ultrasound and told me what to expect, then took me down a long corridor and introduced me to the tech, who I knew because she was my friend's neighbour. And she wasn't just the tech, she also owned the clinic. She lived in a big house with a mature donkey's tail succulent dangling to the floor from a macramé plant hanger in the front window. When weed was legalized she gave my friend a joint to try from an online dispensary she had just started ordering from. My friend and I smoked it in the snow in his yard. We had our parkas on and I made a fire in the firepit. When it kicked in, he had to go inside and sleep. I laughed a lot and went home. I wrote an email to my boss in which I addressed him by the wrong name, only noticed after I sent it, then laughed more. And here I was, standing in front of the tech now with no underwear on, about to have a dead fetus vacuumed out of my body.

They did all kinds of fetuses there. And even though I believe in that, everyone doing what they need to do with their own bodies, in that moment, I couldn't help but resent the cosmological injustice that I didn't get a choice.

The tech tried to get the IV in three times. First in my left hand, then in the crook of my right elbow, then in the crook of my left elbow. She blew out the vein in my hand and shot saline under my skin. I watched as my skin ballooned up and turned blue. Blood squirted out of the back of the syringe as she disconnected the needle. She got a big Band-Aid and covered up the mess. Then she started telling me about her house renovations. About a guy she hired from the clinic, the boyfriend of a patient who she met in that same room: boyfriend off to the side, girlfriend in a mint-green robe. She hired him because she felt sorry for them, she said. He had a contracting company and he was to install marble countertops in her kitchen. She dug around in my right arm like she was trying to get a plumber's snake into a drain.

"He didn't seal the marble," she said. "Seven grand later and he didn't seal the marble."

She told me all about the guy. How sketchy his company was. How long it took. How she always got taken for a ride by contractors because she felt sorry for everyone and wanted to give them money. She asked if I knew anyone who did roofs as she finally slid the IV in on the left side.

I have started bouncing. I bounce as I talk to the other parents at the playgroup and they bounce too. They bounce even if they aren't holding their babies. They bounce and they sway. Their bodies do it without thinking. Everyone is drinking coffee from paper cups and bouncing and swaying. They're young but they all have bags under their eyes and more wrinkles than they did the year before.

They tell me that they've all gone cloth, meaning cloth diapers. They recommend that I join the cloth-diapering group on Facebook. I listen mostly. I change the baby's diaper in the bathroom. It's a disposable. I make shushing noises while I wipe his rolls. He coos. I wrap the diaper up around the wipes and throw it away. I throw away my paper coffee cup. I throw away the peel from my banana. I wash my hands and dry them and throw away the paper towel.

The mothers at the playgroup talk a lot about their baby weight. The thin ones often talk about the weight peeling off when they started breastfeeding. The thin mothers look more tired than the fat mothers. Like their bodies are in need of iron and calories. I can't help but glance when the other mothers breastfeed. I have noticed a lot of variation in areola size and colour and in techniques for discreet nursing. I try to nurse discreetly in public but somehow, I always end up with my whole breast out and my stomach rolls, which still bulge over my pre-pregnancy jeans. I have not purchased breastfeeding shirts with the convenient slit below the breast for discreet nursing. My areolas are pale pink and very large. I wonder if other mothers are comparing shades.

One of the cloth-diapering mothers continues to wear her baby carrier even though she is not carrying her baby. It is a Tula brand carrier, violet with white stars all over it. When I was looking on Marketplace, I had coveted the Tula carriers, but they were more than twice the price of the cheapo ones. The woman's baby is crawling around on the ground and the mother has left the carrier clipped around her hips, with the upper portion and the shoulder straps dangling down by her knees. It's like an apron as the mother stands talking to another mother. They are both swaying and bouncing and drinking coffee. I'm nursing the baby, my breast is all the way out and my stomach is bulging. The baby is sucking greedily, his left hand is stroking my sweater, his eyelids are fluttering and his eyes are rolling back in his head.

In line for my coffee before the group, I wonder what the baby thinks of everyone smiling at him. He must think he is friends with the world. He must think that everyone loves him, that every smile is unconditional love. I feel invisible when I walk with the baby. People do not meet my eye, they look at the baby, they direct comments to me via the baby, in baby talk. There is something liberating about this form of communication.

"Does mummy want a coffee?"

"Where is mummy off to?"

I'm unsure if there is an expectation to answer, I assume there is not.

"Can I have a twelve-ounce coffee?" I say.

"Where is mummy taking you on this sunny day?"

"Is mummy going to the park?"

I try to enjoy disappearing in the interaction. Looking at the baby as he looks at the cashier asking him questions he does not understand. Smiling his toothless smile, drooling, flapping a hand because he has no fine motor skills.

Later that evening when I look at the used cloth diapers for sale on the cloth-diapering group on Facebook, they are ten or even fifteen dollars per diaper and the pinned post on the group advises that twenty diapers is a good number to start with. I'm sitting on the couch I bought at the Salvation Army and the baby is napping beside me, nestled between two pillows with an acrylic crochet blanket around him. The tiny heaviness is resting by the nape of my neck on the back of the couch. Its weight is the same as the weight of the baby and it's warm. It squirms from time to time. I'm comforted by the heaviness, but when I feel it squirm, I'm momentarily repulsed. Like when I first felt the baby move inside my body, a tremor deep in my gut, like I was nervous or cold and then later like part of me was moving, pushing against myself without my consent. If I buy twenty cloth diapers, that means over two hundred dollars up front, which is more than twice what I have in the bank. I get my diapers at Walmart and they cost thirty dollars for a pack of eighty which lasts two weeks. That's sixty dollars a month and that's all I can afford, even though it will cost more in the long run. I can occasionally get more diapers from the food bank and then skip a month of buying diapers.

At the clinic I followed the tech to the operating room and she instructed me to lie down. My gynecologist had his back to me and didn't turn around when I entered. He was doing paperwork. We had already spoken at length when I arrived and I knew he was tired, but eye contact at that point would have been nice, before he reached inside me. It's called a manual aspiration.

In his examination room, earlier, he had described it as a quick suck. As I lay down, I remembered blowing the yolk out of an egg at Easter. Sealing my lips against the chalky shell. Finding the pinhole with my tongue. Blowing hard and feeling the air press back into my jaw and ears until finally the insides gave way and the egg white started oozing out the other end.

There was a TV screen attached to the ceiling. The tech told me it was to help take my mind off things. There was a nature show playing. These spiky lizards interacting in the desert. They were beige and grey with brown speckles. They had sharp spikes down their sides and more spikes that looked like horns on their head. One lizard climbed on top of the other lizard. They were desert horned lizards, also known as horny toads, the subtitles said. The tech attached the fentanyl to the IV and I started to laugh. There was nowhere I would rather have been, nothing I would rather have been watching. I heard the gynecologist swivel around the room on his stool and felt him lift my feet into the stirrups.

"This should only take five minutes," he said.

I felt the speculum go in and the gynecologist said something. I was still laughing and it was coming from deep in my gut. There was a fox on the screen. A lizard was lapping up ants on the sand and the fox was stalking it. It came right over and the lizard ran a bit, its legs like tiny propellers on either side of its body. I felt a pinch.

"I'm removing the remains of conception," the gynecologist said, to no one in particular, or maybe to me. But I was watching the fox trying to smack the lizard with its paws and then there was a close-up of the lizard's eye, which was shut and swelling. The gynecologist stood and left the operating room. I watched as the lizard opened its eye, the lid bulged with pressure, when the eye opened it was just a slit as it shot a sharp spray of blood from the inside corner. The words "reflex bleeding" appeared on the bottom of the screen. The footage was in slow motion and the camera followed the stream of blood as it shot through the air, hitting the fox in the face. My laughter was so intense it reverberated in my chest and I felt tears slipping down my temples. The fox retreated. I noticed something still inside me.

"Is the speculum still in?" I asked.

The gynecologist rushed in and apologized. Click. Slurp.

"It's out," he said.

When I arrive home, I give the baby some food to play with while I cook supper. He is in his high chair and he slaps his yam, smushes it into the tray and into his mouth. The tiny heaviness is on the counter as I chop the onion. My eyes are watering and then the watering makes me cry and I can't tell if the crying is real crying or just watering. The tiny heaviness touches my arm. It is at the table with us. It is on my lap, then it is in my arms. I want to hold it, then I want to push it away. It makes me lose my appetite. I hold the baby instead, he is grunting and does not want to be held but I hold him tighter. The tiny heaviness leaves the room.

As I was leaving the playgroup earlier, I had stopped at the community room for a few minutes to catch the end of a session about sleep training. The room was filled with some of the parents from the playgroup and a lot of people I didn't recognize. Many of them wore Blundstones or Hunter boots, and North Face or MEC or Arc'teryx rain coats. The UPPAbaby stroller seemed to be the preferred stroller. The UPPAbaby Vista or the UPPAbaby Cruz. I looked at those strollers on Amazon, they cost twelve hundred dollars, which is more than my rent.

The sleep consultant talked about crying it out. She said

babies need to learn to self-soothe. She said rocking a baby to sleep is a crutch. She said shushing a baby to sleep is not recommended. She said nursing a baby to sleep is a big no-no. A mother raised her hand and admitted she had been nursing her baby to sleep.

"I really just need my body back," she said. "I don't want to be a human pacifier."

"Three months is a great time to start sleep training," said the trainer.

"I'm feeling over touched," said the mother.

That night in bed, I nurse the baby to sleep, as I do every night. He sleeps in my bed. I get up after the baby and the tiny heaviness fall asleep and leave the door open a crack. I go to the living room, I watch old episodes of Jeopardy on my phone with the volume on low. I make popcorn in the microwave and eat it slowly. Then I crawl back into bed and fall asleep with the baby on one side and the heaviness on the other.

Once the speculum was out, I felt sober. I sat up and asked if I could see the embryo. Blood rushed from my head.

The gynecologist corrected me. "The remains of conception," he said, as he nodded and led me through a door at the other end of the operating room into a tiny lab.

There was a casserole dish full of my tissue on a light table. The dish was not a scientific object and I was confused by it. Like we were in a home economics class, or like we were going to add vinegar to baking soda and watch it explode. I have the same casserole dish in my kitchen. One of the small square Pyrex ones. Mine has golden grease stains on the sides and handles. This one was impeccably clean. It was filled with saline and bits of blood and tissue. The gynecologist and the tech were hunched over the light table. They both had black lamps attached to their heads and they were wearing long white lab coats. The gynecologist's tiny spotlight shone on the bits of frayed flesh that she pulled from the casserole dish with a pair of tweezers and placed carefully into two different urine sample bottles, also filled with saline.

"We're trying to get as much sample material as possible," he said. "To get good results." I leaned right in to get a closer look. It looked just like my period. Small round clots suspended in water, strands of mucus, bits of pink, paper-thin tissue. There was not a lot. Surprisingly little. He pointed to one clump. "This is what we're looking for," he said. "Stuff that looks like it made up the sac."

I felt dizzy, I thought I might faint and I said something like "cool" or "wow." The tech looked up at me, her light shining in my eyes as I squinted at her. She lifted her glasses onto her head.

"Do you want to see a picture of a miscarried embryo from earlier today?" she asked. "Fully intact."

"Yes," I said, for reasons I cannot explain. Or maybe I know exactly why. Maybe it was because I wanted to witness the universe that had opened inside me. See what that brief world had looked like before it had disappeared. Understand the precariousness of a cluster of cells as life. See what had been my future before it ceased to belong to me.

She took out her phone and scrolled. Slid her thumb and forefinger apart on the screen to zoom right in. Then passed it to me. I took the phone and looked at the little tail. The arm buds. The bulbous head. The bulging eye. The light from the tech's headlamp glinted off the screen, then, as I handed the phone back, it was directly in my eyes. For just a moment all I could see was the white of the light.

I wake and my T-shirt is hiked up above my breasts. The baby is rooting for my nipple. I think I hear something in the kitchen. I don't feel the tiny heaviness in the bed. I sit up with the baby in my arms nursing and listen but it's all silent. I put the baby down and he squirms, eyes still closed. I get out of bed and pull the curtain back on the window. The street is empty, it is just before dawn and still dark. Hazy purple rises above the hills across the harbour, the lights from the boats are glittering, the street lights are still on, and the street below is glowing orange. The baby is gurgling and the gurgling is getting louder as he wakes up and realizes I'm not there. I walk down the hall. My feet are freezing on the cold hardwood. I open the front door a crack and peer out onto the landing. The lights are bright. I hear the door to the building open and then close loudly. I rush back to the bedroom, leaving the door to my apartment ajar. The baby is crying now and out the window I see the shadow of the old woman from downstairs going down the steps, through the front yard, past the gate and into the street. She walks down the street slowly and then stops and looks up at my window. I let the curtain fall into place and look at the baby, who is searching for me, his eyes are open and he starts crying, his head turning from side to side. I notice the absence of the heaviness as I take the baby in my arms and hug him close. He stops crying, roots, sucks, his eyelids flutter. I hear the front door click closed. I feel a weight lift.

lost villages

JIM MCEWEN

And dark and drunk and damp . . . and Dad asked for me to drag the dead deer to the ditch and I was drunk.

Now I remember that old world. Sinking then into the dark, in those mumbling fantasies moments before falling asleep about if only stories could be changed. Retrieve the dew on the hay stems, along the old furrows, through the bramble and burr, the donkeys braying and the milkweed's floss. Here was Dad's quiet fathersome request and then the deer viscera. And here after Dad and the deer, the road at twilight—away and always hungry, desirous down the side roads, accelerating directly at the purple sinful moon. Alive and driving our lives all the way to a great betrayal on the other side of the planet. All that, all that era of hope and fooling, both boots with soakers, nights starrier and drunk as hell.

Drag the dead deer then. To the ditch.

I studied the deer. It was very small and pleasant, this pleasing soft and long-eyelashed doe, however some of the insides were opened and presented with flies collecting. I held one hoof, revulsed. This was in the back field near the hauntings of the abandoned farmhouse and the pulled-up train tracks. Dad worried the coyotes would find her and tear her all over and as well it wouldn't do; it wasn't right to have her in the middle of the field as she was. He would have dragged the deer if Grampa told him. And Grampa, who fought alcoholism and depression and The Depression and the Wehrmacht, leaving aside those coyotes, would have dragged the deer too. I wrinkled my nose and said I would handle this later. I was required at a Halloween party, not such embarrassing business with Dad and the deer. This is true.

I don't think we were bad boys, not too bad, but we were certainly boys. Once we thought we took such great bites out of day and night. We were making our stories. We were told to go to university and not get anyone pregnant or become plumbers. We were told we killed all the polar bears and old forests and to recycle. We were told to sit and express ourselves and have a plan, that we were all special and to find something we loved doing. We should have had a war, but we surely would have lost it. My friends, my closest friends, were MacKinnon, McKenzie and Cooney, everyone by our last names like we were hockey players, like we were important men. We took turns forsaking each other. Sometimes I loved them, sometimes I wondered if I had antisocial personality disorder.

On the evening of the big Katherine, Katherine, Kathryn, Catherine, and Brandon's Halloween house party in town, MacKinnon and McKenzie were waiting in the laneway in an absolutely mangled-to-shit old car, one door a different colour and the grill fortified with chicken wire. One of them, I don't remember which, had creamed a deer of his own, and now sometimes the hood would fly open on the highway, wholly obstructing the driver's view of the road, which was always alarming and very dangerous. McKenzie and MacKinnon waved at Dad, who was wheeling around wheelbarrows of wood and dirt. And I came out from the fields, having not dragged the deer, and thinking not about the deer but something else, something Sarah P., whom I was supposed to be dating, not Sarah B., whom everyone wanted to date, had said to me. She said one day I might figure it out. We were lying in her bed and we talked about drama class, and horses giving birth, and first blowjobs, and so on, and then this something I was supposed to figure out which she seemed to have already figured out. She laughed, lying across me in her bed. One day maybe, she said. I felt along her skin. I still can't remember what I'm supposed to figure out one day.

McKenzie put the pedal down past cornfields and the cows, he overtook a tractor and a hay wagon, and MacKinnon opened a camping cooler. It was full of liquors and mix. I mean not bottles and ice, but a cooler full to the top with a little stinky purple ocean with waves breaking into surf against the sides. I had an open beer but he took it and dumped it in too, then gave me a cup of this mess which I spilt all over myself, focussed as I was on what looked to be a man way off down a flat, yellow field shooting at a goose. We were boys charioting a rotten pile of liquor past corn and hay and goose hunts and dusk.

We arrived at Cooney's house to drink before the party because his village was on the way to town. I believe this was grade 12 and we fancied ourselves tough and cool enough to go to a party held by all these people who'd graduated high school already and left our township and lived in a humongous and old house full of mice near the university in town.

Cooney wasn't in a conversational mood. He'd eaten some

strange drugs from the future that didn't have a name yet, just letters and numbers. A puzzle held his attention. The box said five hundred pieces and it was a farm scene with cows, chickens and a red barn. It was finished, but Cooney held one more piece up. He held it so it seemed like what he was holding was of grave importance.

An extra piece?

Or . . . you could say . . . that it only took me 499 pieces to complete a 500-piece puzzle, he said slowly, gazing into the distance.

Let's go outside, said MacKinnon after a time.

McKenzie peed on an elm tree with a cigarette tight in his teeth.

Oh I'm feeling a dirty one tonight, he said.

It will be a fine party.

We should get dressed up.

Bah, said MacKinnon.

But McKenzie had a packet of face paint and we drew on kitty faces with smudged whiskers, laughing into the mirror. We searched for something to fashion into ears. And then Cooney emerged from the basement wearing a spectacular raccoon costume. He seemed oblivious to his incredible transformation and paused and stared right back at us.

Eh? he said.

I said, Outstanding.

He looked down at his paws and turned, which made his tail swing. This old thing?

We filled grocery bags with his dad's Molson Drys—his father drank so much that he hopefully wouldn't notice if forty-eight bottles were missing from his garage-ful of Molson Dry inventory.

At the party Sarah P. ignored me and then she was kissing

with Brandon. This is probably fine, I thought. Cooney went missing and I drank a lot of cold beer very quickly. I found my friend Ricky Murder, an obese amateur rapper with a cleft palate, and his girlfriend, whom we called Becky Murder. They didn't have any weed or ecstasy to sell or share. McKenzie talked to an uninterested Sarah B. with his fly down and MacKinnon, who adored wizards and wizardry, trailed a small and annoyed wizard through the party, explaining to him that he was the most bitch-ass wizard he'd ever seen. And so she goes, me and my shameful cohort.

I was drunk and high then, having an embarrassing conversation with someone I was pretending I knew and cared about, waiting patiently in the lineup for the bathroom to do drugs. McKenzie surprised me with a savage punch in the bag.

Sarah B., not Sarah P., was gliding through this party looking bored and gorgeous as always, wearing a tiny "I Love NY" T-shirt. Cooney reanimated behind me, his raccoon costume now filthy (he told me later he believed he truly was a raccoon for a few hours because of the experimental drugs and so had been sorting through the garbage under the sink).

New York is my favourite city, he said, he who'd never been on a plane but once drove to Brockville.

And state, said I.

Sarah B. did not turn her head. This may have been the party where she talked Cooney into tricking two poor fellows who were pestering her into drinking urine. And not simply sipping on it but powerfully beer-funnelling about a litre of human urine into their stomachs in an instant. Imagine one moment there's no pee in your stomach, the next, there's a lot of it in there. Maybe this is too gross though, if it happened at all, and I'll try to relate it another time.

But I do remember Cooney rocking back and forth, this great

dying raccoon smeared with yoghurt and cigarette butts and garbage particles, looking at me and saying: you're lucky your dad is yours. I see him now, my memories mixing, his raccoon fur imbued with trash-water and urine and kimchi, although of course that's not right. Later he would betray me, but that's for later. And I'd always betrayed him by not talking to the guidance counsellor about his dad.

You're lucky your dad is yours, he repeats.

While he spoke, a bottle smashed upstairs, there was much shouting and MacKinnon slid on his back perfectly out cold down the entire flight of stairs. He came to a rest in the alcove with an arm across his face. The little wizard had taken enough abuse and put all sorts of wizardry into his punch.

Of course there was a fight—there has to be a fight. We were terrible at fighting. McKenzie and MacKinnon enjoyed fights but lost almost all of them. I was quite useless and would only get involved if I was blackout drunk, and then normally I just fell over and hoped my pants stayed up. Cooney was interesting because he was strong from summers on the farm and if he got angry, well it was a bloodbath—such that once an onlooker threw up from all the blood, so rattled was he at the gore and hell Cooney brought down on an unlucky lad from Stittsville who really had it coming in the parking lot at the arena. But that was rare. His conditions and addictions, diagnoses and tricky home life came out in funny ways. He cried, I recall he cried in the rain while paused to look at a faded, disintegrating lost cat poster stapled to a telephone pole of a very old cat, "Sampson," who'd been missing over a year. Cooney tried to hide that he was crying and I pretended I didn't see.

Katherine, Katherine, Kathryn, Catherine, and Brandon tried then to marshal some order into their party that had taken a turn. Pushing and pleading in the hallway, and Ricky Murder was so big in the hallway and getting in everyone's way. Brandon was wearing a dragon costume and he yelled at me about my friends' behaviour. Then Cooney seized Brandon's dragon tail and tried to pull it off. MacKinnon stirred and McKenzie was on the warpath.

McKenzie was out into the street now, and he got very upset and had his chest pushed out. He addressed the house in a roar.

We're not leaving—until someone comes out—and fights me!

The wizard's tiny head in his wizarding cap was visible for a moment on the balcony.

You! McKenzie bellowed, and he pointed.

Please just leave! cried all the Katherines up on the balcony. Leave!

But we did not leave, and then the front door exploded open, cracking the hinges, to reveal an enormous and fit young lad with a necklace and a good haircut. The wizard had sent his champion. The man cleared the steps in a bound, headed straight for McKenzie and delivered a ferocious boot right on his forehead.

Down went McKenzie, crumpled wordlessly onto the sidewalk, the man fell on him and I fell on the man and him. I aimed to punch the man right in his good haircut but instead struck McKenzie in his spinal column between his shoulder blades. He gurgled away beneath me with this pile of people on top of him and the man swung at me, didn't miss, and I felt his ring tear my cheek, tear my kitten whiskers. Mercifully then, this terrifying, fit young man, this berserker, whoever this was, he complained he had to throw up so he stopped fighting. Why not just throw up on us? I wondered. And in summation, Ricky Murder put him in a headlock, twisting his head like he was trying to open a bottle of pop, and threw him down in the road. After that Ricky Murder smashed all the pumpkins in front of the house while lisping and rapping to himself about how Ricky Murder smashed all the pumpkins in front of the house.

A neighbour walking his dog said, and I remember this clearly, he said that the whole ordeal was the stupidest thing he'd ever seen.

But what in the frig am I talking about—what is all this? I feel cold. Looking at this now.

Maybe it's to show—we were here . . . primates dancing at the end of a civilization, the deer undragged in those eager and rabid days before the cellphone and before the frontal lobe. Or, just a small drinking-story laugh in the darkness before we forget everything.

Cooney read some of the stories.

Well I like it, he said. Maybe it's because I know you, but sure I like it.

We should have all just gone to bed, I said.

You have any idea the drunk stories my dad could have told? I think he murdered someone.

Then he remarked: Imagine getting shit from your girlfriend because you're hungover and you say, listen babe, now I drank a lot of piss last night all right, lay off me . . .

I was holding his youngest daughter, who was six months old. It was like holding a tiny sun or energy source of sorts. She squealed and sang to herself, turning her head this way and that way to investigate and wonder at her world. She whimpered then laughed and put her face in her hands. Her new skin, her minute eyelashes—she had the heart rate and rapid breathing pattern of I assume a mouse and she even smelled wonderful. What she smelled like was hope.

Cooney was exhausted, a great pillow-crease up one side of his face like a scar, tidying up all the barf-cloths, and stumbling around many deflating balloons from a birthday party. We discussed pleasure and pain. As in, is everything we do an attempt to have pleasure and/or avoid pain?

Yes, I think so, he said. He leaned against the washing machine full of barf and cloths and craned his head up at the ceiling. It's just—well it's just pleasure changes, from say oh . . . snorting coke off a pack of darts in Bells Corners—to being able to look your father in the eyes. *Your* father at least.

I bounced the baby.

Or no, hold on, he said. They're the same thing. Pleasure is pain. There's no pleasure without pain. You think about it—anything that's actually pleasure, pleasurable, has to come through the pain.

I offered the baby a plastic toy ear of corn with the John Deere logo on it that vibrated her gums when she clamped it in her little mouth and drooled all over it.

Eh? said Cooney. Dating, frigging doing hard work and not failing or getting big muscles or—and he pointed at his baby. He was pleased with his revelation.

It's gotta hurt so good, I said.

Yes, he said. Yes, if it's only pleasure then we're all five-hundred-pound monsters beating off everywhere with immense anxiety disorders. Put that in your stories there buddy.

Cooney by the grace of God had sorted out all his addictions and tumults and surprised everyone by becoming a rich, overworked real estate lawyer. This is funny because in grade 12 law class he ripped my test out of my hands to cheat off it when Mrs. Gagnon had her back turned, and I tried to rip my test back out of his hands and he shouted what! and then we ripped the test in half and Mrs. Gagnon turned and shouted at us. He got married, to an absolute missile launcher of a babe, and now they have three daughters. Also he got invisible braces—finally rich enough to fix his shitty, poor-kid teeth.

MacKinnon did a year and a day at the jailhouse on Innes Road then went to the oil patch.

McKenzie was distant and withdrawn in the years after high school—he lived with his mum on Line 3 and delivered pizzas and said he didn't want to talk to anyone. He said he was going to kill himself and then he did, in his room in the basement with mason jars of urine and his video game character just standing there on the computer screen.

And I drag around these stories and the shame, and try not to lie, and remember, if anyone cares these little notes and bits begging towards redemption.

Here are some examples from my notes:

-All books should have maps at the start.

-The day the cows escaped / And reclaimed the football field / At the high school.

-Good words: Samovar. Acumen. Stenographer.

-Bad words: Zeitgeist. Imbue.

-Can we retire the word juxtapose please?

-I asked Grampa if he'd ever been to Bar le Whip, the legendary horse-betting bar on the Quebec side, and he glared into the distance and said, No—but I've threatened to.

-In the Oligocene, birds ate horses.

Grampa came from a village that's now an underwater ghost town. One of those Lost Villages of Eastern Ontario that were evacuated and submerged to make way for the St. Lawrence Seaway in 1958. Once we took him in a motorboat and floated him over his hometown. He looked down over the gunwales and saw his old sidewalks and church foundations. He said he didn't want to see it again after that.

He was deeply puzzled by a kiwi and needed convincing to try it. If he was going to be in the hospital a long time, he said, pull the plug, pull the plug—under no circumstances are you to not pull the plug. Hunting, to him, meant driving his truck down the side roads and across the fields, driving while rolling his cigarette, opening his beer and loading his shotgun, all in perfect skilful concert, and rolling down the window to shoot a partridge. Only he knew how to start his old Chevy six-cylinder and I watched, as a boy, fascinated while Grampa swore quietly and wiped his hands, the truck coughing exhaust, out on the edge of death, but then the engine finally turning over and finding the deep growl.

You hear that? He took my hand. That's the sound that won the war.

When he was very old, we went on a family trip to the War Museum for Father's Day. And they had one of Hitler's cars in there, a magnificent and huge old stretched Rolls Royce. Grampa ignored the signs and ropes around the car and went and sat in it. He looked very content, sitting in the back there—I got your car you bastard, after all these years—and then an alarm went off and museum staff coaxed him out of the car.

If I fought that bastard I should be able to sit in his car, he explained.

When he died we gave the undertaker his matching sweatshirt and sweatpants from Giant Tiger to put on him and had him cremated in a particleboard coffin with yellow polymer rope handles.

Cooney asked if I was going to put our Korean misadventures into the story.

Oh Lord, I said.

But we were scoundrels, and Cooney's idea of fleeing to Korea to teach ESL was obviously superior to setting up scaffolding in Smiths Falls when it was minus thirty and going deaf on construction sites, getting drunk at Junior B games and owing a lot of people money. This was during the recession and everyone was skedaddling off somewhere, anywhere. You needed a degree, and I had a one, great bona fide help that it was, and Cooney forged his, in communication studies from Laurentian University.

He proved to be a poor flyer, as I expected. His first airplane a fourteen-hour shot, shaking and rattling the hours away with ballooning sinuses and pressure-treated skulls over the Bering Sea, and he continually dug out his annoying suitcase, bumping me with his knee or elbow, to make sure all his touches of home and good-luck charms were in proper order. He was not taking this well and tried to sleep with his head on my shoulder. We packed all our problems from the New World in our suitcases as well.

And unsure what day it was, whether we were in the future or the past, we descended on the polite and good nation, on the bullet trains, down the sleepless halogened alleys. Now kimchi is truly delicious, the cellphones wizardly, streets crime-free, good Samaritans all over peeling drunk comatose foreigners such as us off the roads. The schoolchildren in their blazers and their skirts were so profoundly kind and adorable and smart it's difficult to process or describe. I recall a particular grade 4 girl helping a less fortunate child with her English word-search, and I smiled and she smiled, with her entire pristine and holy soul bursting out of her little face, and I froze, not knowing how to react to a visit from an angel, except perhaps by having a nervous breakdown.

We were there almost two months before they kicked us out permanently. I believe the whole peninsula cheered.

The bars never closed and we made friends with other insomniac boozers from all corners of the Anglosphere, places such as Birmingham, Durban, Auckland, Newfoundland and Michigan. We stayed in love motels—tiny rooms with a single bed, Kleenex, lubricant, soft-core pornos, and an overhead red light that wouldn't turn off—which were rented by the hour. Cooney got lost and arrived at the love motel late, holding the decapitated body of a massive stuffed-toy bear he won at a Korean fair and wearing the bear's head for a hat. There were already maybe three people in the bed and no more blankets, so he lay down on the floor and pulled stuffing out of the bear's body cavity to arrange on himself in lieu of a blanket. In the bleak red morning he looked just like a dirty old cumulonimbus cloud on the floor.

Soon, of course, Cooney began to order drugs off the internet. Of course he did this. Korea was not a smart place to have drugs, and the jail times for drugs were sizable. He was fond of Russian synthetic herbal ecstasy tablets, also called benzylpiperazine, also called BZP. Pills of fake happiness from some distant and dismal oblast. It was more like very, very shitty speed than ecstasy. Your pupils go huge and peeing becomes a difficult and piping-hot task and you talk seriously and loudly about nonsense for hours.

They ship them right to the school! Cooney said, overjoyed. I also ordered some dick-pills, he continued.

Do you need dick-pills?

No. I don't think so, I dunno buddy.

I too ordered a fifty-pill BZP shipment.

I told Cooney, not to worry, that I'd fictionalize him.

Yeah feel free to call me . . . he thought. Like, Morley, uh Morley . . . Ratman. Morley "Snitch" Ratman.

Okay, I said.

I really should have died, he said.

Sleeping in love motels with alcoholic British strangers, or in drunk tanks, or on the road, it's impossible not to be reminded of one's warm and small childhood bed. When I was a boy Dad would put a chair by the bed and read all the proper books, dinosaur books, horsemanship books, then Anne Frank's diary and *Who Has Seen the Wind* and more, and change his voice for the King and the Duke, Cousin Dill, Tom Robinson, or terrifying old Pew, and all these characters patrolled my bedscape long after I fell into my dreams. He thought a boy should know these books. When he was a boy Grampa told him nothing mattered because the Russians were gonna nuke everything anyway.

When I got in trouble, that meant stacking wood crying or getting sent to my room crying, but at least not getting kicked while crying, like Cooney's experiences. And in my room, I'd cry until I had a headache and savour how bad Dad would feel if I ran away, then fall asleep before supper. Sometimes he'd bring my supper to my room to say he was sorry for overreacting. I'd pretend to be asleep with my back turned, tears dried to salt, wanting to stay mad, but wanting him to read to me as well. I felt him standing there, paused with the plate. He left after a while and the green beans went cold and curling on the plate on the night table.

So Morley "Snitch" Ratman ratted on me. He gave me up.

Ratman's big shipment arrived before mine did. He came to

my apartment, struggling to fit his cartoon eyeballs through the doorway.

I brought you something to tide you over, he said. He put a small jar with two pills in it in the fridge door. I'm not sure why in the fridge.

I was gonna wait till the weekend, when I'm drunk, I said.

Oh sure no trouble, he said.

Then we went public ice-skating at the only rink in town, with some Korean girls, and Ratman enjoyed himself immensely, flying around with his hands behind his back, full of BZP tablets and possibly dick-pills.

When my pills came, I put the parcel in the main compartment of the fridge, then went on a blind date at a chicken restaurant, where Ratman called me on what was maybe my third Korean cellphone, because I kept losing them, and he asked me where I was.

We did eventually leave that Halloween party, after tiring of Ricky Murder's pumpkin-raps and shepherding Cooney away from the garbage he was digging through on the curb. Now he wore just the bottom half of the raccoon costume, and he ate a waterlogged donut off the sidewalk, like a good raccoon.

The highway got dark and cold and rotten, and then half an hour down a darker road and I began to feel terrible about not dragging the deer. I mumbled about dragging the dead deer. I should have done as Dad said. And also Sarah P. had figured something out I had not.

We unpacked grimy old Cooney onto his lawn and then McKenzie continued driving with half his brain hanging out from the boot he took to the head. I sat in the back and MacKinnon sat in the passenger seat.

Well lads should we have one more line then? asked McKenzie.

Oh, oh I don't feel very good . . . said MacKinnon.

McKenzie looked at the road, at MacKinnon, then back to the road, trying to keep 'er between the ditches. We were on my road now, almost at my house.

Please . . . no don't throw up, McKenzie said, and immediately a large bird burst on the windshield, burst to bits, and the biggest bit slid off slowly right in front of MacKinnon, these bloody wings, feathers and twitching foot, open beak and one dead bird eye eying MacKinnon. He gave McKenzie a hopeless look, and then burst himself, loud wet barf all down between his feet.

Will you drop me at the top of the laneway I don't wanna wake up my folks I gotta go find the deer! I said.

Eh, said McKenzie. He tugged MacKinnon's leg out of the way to look at the barf.

I gotta drag a dead deer! I said and I shut the door. I went out into the dark purple field to do my job. I was full of beer and cocaine and valour.

I couldn't hear Morley "Snitch" Ratman very well on my third, or even fourth, cellphone.

What? I said. Eh? Buddy, hold the phone closer to your head. Where are you . . .

I'm at a restaurant. I can't hear anything.

What restaurant? He wasn't holding the phone any closer to his head.

The uh, the chicken one. You know the chicken one.

He hung up. My date didn't show up.

Then Ratman called ten minutes later and asked me to come out.

I came out of the restaurant quite grumpy and then it wasn't Ratman who met me at all, but instead two plainclothes police officers with an interpreter. The officers were stern although not rough, and they put me in handcuffs.

The interpreter said, did Mr. Ratman give you some medicine? He said he gave you some medicine.

I thought for a minute then said, yes. He did.

Ratman sat in the back seat of a police car and they put me in next to him. His face was red and I could tell he'd been crying.

For some thoroughly peculiar reason I transcended all of this to a higher and calmer state. I knew everything would be okay—which is insane. Just get it over with, I thought. I even felt a little annoyed, as in could we wrap this up please, I'd like to go smoke some darts.

Ratman told me later when he was sitting there in the back seat of the police car, he'd been imagining ways to kill himself in jail. He was not calm. He welled up again and so much drool came out of his mouth. He said he was sorry he was a rat. Over and over.

I don't know, maybe I would have done the same, I said.

At the police station, an officer had all the dirty little pills lined up in a row on his keyboard as he, perplexed and squinting, researched BZP on the computer.

Our interpreter stayed with us. Maybe he was in his thirties but it was hard to tell, very thin, forever beaming and grinning and winking away. A truly fine and warm man in a shiny silver suit with a purple tie.

You rascals! He said, chuckling some more and gripping Ratman's shoulder. Rascals!

Are we going to die, said Ratman.

I am Oh Kyoung-su and I am your interpreter, he said,

pointing at his chest. Do you like Toronto?

Yes, Ratman lied, dismayed. Let's go Leafs, he said with his face in his hands.

Slowly our fate came for us down through the halls. The police officers conferenced. For eight hours they kept us in the room.

In the end, what saved us was Wikipedia, Canadian law concerning BZP, and a translator computer program called Babel Fish. They let Ratman use the police station computer, and he was much better at the computer than I, and he produced a Wikipedia page showing BZP was legal in Canada. Or probably it was so new that Canada didn't have a law for it yet, whereas everything was forbidden in Korea. They didn't want their young people turning out like us. Devils that we were. Ratman then implemented the Babel Fish program to translate the Wikipedia page into Korean to prove the story he was going with—that he'd been taking medicine for his stress and anxiety, which was legal in his land.

Kyoung-su was indefatigable and consoled Ratman. I asked Kyoung-su why he was helping us.

This happens when the foreigners get in trouble. The policemen need someone to speak in English. It's . . . I volunteered. He took off his glasses and scratched the back of his head. His suit was so shiny and stiff it could hardly have been comfortable.

And later he said: when I was your age I was in Toronto, Ontario. I got in trouble—too much beer you know. My English was not so good and the interpreter man helped me at the police station. So, I help here.

Kyoung-su was an angel from the Lord.

Ratman was asleep then on the floor like a cat. I stood over him and watched, to check that he was breathing. The room was white, cold and still.

He's fucked, I said pointing down at Ratman at my feet. I'm okay. Can they let him go? He has a very poor father figure and he's addicted to just about everything.

But the door opened and the police officers were back with their decision. Ratman sprang up off the floor. On the other side of the earth, in this strange and faraway room, so far from our sleeping township, I already knew everything would be all right while he did not. One of the police officers said something to Kyoung-su, then turned to face us silently. Kyoung-su nodded and bowed. He put his hands together, intertwining his fingers, his eyes sparkling and glittery behind his glasses.

No jail, he said. You are very lucky.

Just a beautiful bouquet of sparkling, grinning, winks and head-shaking. He laughed and shook my hand. I could not wait to go smoke darts with him on the dark concrete police station steps.

Oh! said Ratman, and he slithered back on the floor.

Now we only have to go back to your apartment to get the medicine that Mr. Ratman gave to you, Kyoung-su said.

Oh, I said. Back?

And I never found the deer. The coyotes got her. I did find one ear. I wandered wet and defeated in the hayfield and the barn birds brought a pale dawn. I felt the ear, very flappy and soft; my inclination was to pocket it. The coyotes had dragged the deer all over, edited her down to one downy brown ear.

Still I wasn't sober, not exactly, and I wanted to do something brave and the only thing brave to do, I believed, was to go into the abandoned and haunted farmhouse at the back. Up over the fence then and across the old train tracks, treading in a dream down the lane and past the creek and rusting tangles of old farming machinery, up a pile of bricks in front of the house, swaying and stumbling, and the door fell off. I cut my hand on a nail and went in and just sat in the farmhouse for a while, ready to take whatever hauntings might come.

There was a bathtub sunk through the lath and plaster that had landed in the summer kitchen. Lots of shotgun shells and bullet-holes leaking the dusty sun. Little trees pierced up through the floorboards. Bowls of rust and dust, a can with a faded label on the stove—the last supper. It looks like they left in a hurry. I recognized a decaying wheelchair from childhood nightmares. I sat down and let the ghosts shiver along my back.

The police officers had already been to my apartment, led by Ratman, and they'd looked everywhere for the medicine. But not in the fridge.

Kyoung-su said, please give to them the medicine. Then he went to the corner, picked up my hockey stick, held it and smiled to himself.

I opened the fridge, to the groans of the police officers, took the little jar with two pills from the door, gave it to the police officers, closed the fridge that also contained my parcel with fifty pills in it, and stood in front of it. My hands behind my back touching the cool fridge. The pills had happiness in them.

After and alone, I did not flush them down the toilet. That would be lying. I shut the curtains, locked the door, sat on the floor and shook all the powder from all the capsules into a small Ziploc bag, tried to bury the bag on a mountain the next day but worried I was being watched, then hid the bag in my tub of laundry detergent.

Two weeks later we had to leave Korea and never come back.

Back in the hayfield, away from the farmhouse, away from the ghosts and finally ready for bed, I could see Dad in his nightgown and rubber boots, with the dog, up to get the paper at the road. So he didn't see me, I sat down in all the dew on the hay, holding the one soft ear. That awful feeling you can never fully remember what's been lost and sunken away. The green beans gone cold on the plate. He looked tired, walking back down the laneway with the paper and the dog. And still he walks, past and away from me, and right off the page.

about the authors

Lisa Moore is the author of *This Is How We Love*, *Degrees of Nakedness*, *Open*, *Alligator*, *February*, *Caught*, *Something for Everyone*, and the young adult novel *Flannery*. She lives in St. John's where she is a professor of creative writing at Memorial University.

Xaiver Michael Campbell is a writer, baker, and outdoor enthusiast. He is originally from Jamaica and now lives in St. John's. Xaiver's work has appeared in *Riddle Fence*, the *Malahat Review*, and *Us, Now* (Breakwater, 2021).

Bridget Canning has published two novels: *The Greatest Hits of Wanda Jaynes* (2017) and *Some People's Children* (2020). In 2019, she won the CBC Emerging Artist Award with ArtsNL. Her first short story collection, *No One Knows about Us*, will be published with Breakwater Books in 2022. She holds a MA in creative writing from Memorial University and a master of literacy education from Mount Saint Vincent University. She grew up in Highlands, Newfoundland and Labrador, and currently lives in St. John's.

Prajwala Dixit is an author, journalist, documentary filmmaker, and theatre practitioner whose works have been produced and published by local and national organizations that include NFB, the *Globe and Mail*, the *National Post*, *POV*, *JSource*, *Newfoundland Quarterly*, the Arts and Culture Centre (NL), RCAT, and Artistic

Fraud. Winner of the Arts and Letters Award and silver finalist at the Atlantic Journalism Awards, Prajwala calls Bengaluru and St. John's home, where she lives with her family, consuming stories through film and books.

Terry Doyle is from the Goulds, Newfoundland. His first book, *DIG*, was a finalist for the Danuta Gleed Literary Award, the Newfoundland and Labrador Book Award for Fiction, the ReLit Award for Fiction, the Margaret and John Savage First Book Award for Fiction, and the Alistair MacLeod Prize for Short Fiction. His first novel, *The Wards*, is available now.

Benjamin C. Dugdale is a poet and experimental filmmaker from Rural Alberta (Treaty 7 Territory). B's writing can be found in places like *GEIST*, *Plenitude*, and *giallo*. In 2021, B completed their SSRHC-funded MA in creative writing at Memorial University. Their most recent film, *Contents under Pressure*, is distributed by the CFMDC. Their full-length debut (a book-length poem), *The Repoetic: After Saint Pol Roux*, is available from Gordon Hill Press in Spring 2023.

Allison Graves received her BA in English literature from Dalhousie University and her MA in creative writing from Memorial University, where she wrote a collection of short stories called *Soft Serve*—forthcoming with Breakwater Books. Her fiction has won *Room* magazine's annual fiction contest and the Newfoundland Arts and Letters Award. She is a fiction editor of *Riddle Fence*. She is doing a PhD at Memorial and likes to play drums and climb Signal Hill.

Carmella Gray-Cosgrove is from Vancouver and has lived in St. John's for twelve years. Her writing has appeared in *PRISM International*, *Broken Pencil*, the *New Quarterly*, and elsewhere. Her debut short story collection, *Nowadays and Lonelier*, won the BMO Winterset Award and was shortlisted for the NLCU Fresh

Fish Award for Emerging Writers. Carmella is a fiction editor at *Riddle Fence*.

Elizabeth Hicks is a writer, actor, and filmmaker from Newfoundland. She holds an MA in English from Memorial University. As a playwright, Elizabeth has been commissioned by Poverty Cove Theatre, Artistic Fraud, and Persistence Theatre. Elizabeth and her work have appeared in *Riddle Fence* magazine, at the St. John's International Women's Film Festival, on stages across Newfoundland and Labrador, and at sketch comedy festivals in Toronto, Chicago, and New York City.

Matthew Hollett is a writer and photographer in St. John's. *Optic Nerve*, a collection of poems about photography and visual perception, is forthcoming from Brick Books in 2023. His first book, *Album Rock* (2018), is a work of creative nonfiction and poetry investigating a curious photo taken in Newfoundland in the 1850s. Matthew won the 2020 CBC Poetry Prize for a poem about walking the Lachine Canal during the early days of the pandemic. He is working on a novel.

Tzu-Hao Hsu was born in Taiwan and raised in Newfoundland. A proud Taiwanese Townie, she is a business manager by day and creative soul by night. This is her second publication with Breakwater, and she is grateful for the opportunity to contribute to the evolving tapestry of contemporary Newfoundland literature. Tzu-Hao lives in St. John's with her husband, twin daughters, and two beagles, and she regularly chronicles her parenting adventures on social media for stress relief and a laugh.

Jim McEwen grew up in Dunrobin, Ontario. He is a graduate of the English and creative writing master's program at Memorial University and winner of the Cuffer Prize (2015) and the Leaside Fiction Contest (2019). His first novel, *Fearnoch*, is out now with Breakwater Books.

ABOUT THE AUTHORS

William Ping is a Chinese Canadian novelist and journalist. He has won the 2022 Cox & Palmer Creative Writing Award and the 2021 Landfall Trust Award and was named a Fellow of Memorial University's School of Graduate Studies. His work has previously been featured on CBC, in *Riddle Fence*, and in *Us, Now* (Breakwater, 2021). His debut novel, *Hollow Bamboo*, received Memorial's Department of English Award for Thesis Excellence and will be published in Winter 2023 by HarperCollins Canada.

Michelle Porter is a writer and scholar who was born on the Métis homeland and is now living in Newfoundland and Labrador. She is the descendent of a long line of Métis storytellers. Many of her ancestors (the Goulet family) told stories using music, and today she tells stories using the written word. She is the author of *Approaching Fire*, *Scratching River*, and the forthcoming novel, *A Grandmother Begins the Story* (Penguin, 2023). Her first book of poetry, *Inquiries*, was shortlisted for the Pat Lowther Memorial Award for Best Book of Poetry, Canada (2019) and was a finalist for the E. J. Pratt Poetry Award (2021). She teaches creative writing at Memorial University.

Olivia Robinson is originally from the Annapolis Valley, Nova Scotia, and currently lives in Charlottetown, Prince Edward Island, with her tuxedo cat, Puss. She completed her BA in English at UPEI and her MA in creative writing at Memorial University. Her first novel, *The Blue Moth Motel*, was published in October 2021 with Breakwater Books. Her work has also appeared in *Riddle Fence* and the *UPEI Arts Review*. In addition to writing, Olivia works as a bookseller.

Sobia Shaheen Shaikh is a mother, writer, activist, social work professor, and engaged community member from St. John's, Newfoundland and Labrador. She has deep community ties with anti-racist, feminist, arts, women's, disability, youth, student, and environmental justice organizations across Canada, and especially in Newfoundland and Labrador. Sobia is a founding member of the Anti-Racism Coalition NL, the Quilted Collective of Racialized NL Writers, and the Creators' Collective NL: Indigenous, Racialized and Migrant Artists and Arts Workers.

Heidi Wicks has written for CBC, the *Newfoundland Quarterly*, *Riddle Fence,* the *Globe and Mail*, and Breakwater Books' creative nonfiction anthology *Best Kind* (2018). Her debut novel, *Melt* (Breakwater, 2020), made the *Globe and Mail*'s Best Summer Reading list in 2020. She recently received ArtsNL funding to complete a short story collection, titled *Here*. Her *Hard Ticket* story was inspired by Tom Wolfe's *Electric Kool-Aid Acid Test* and a lifelong regret of never attending Salmon Festival.

Carrie-Jane Williams is from the St. John's community of Goulds. After many wonderful and unpredictable years of teaching English-language learners across Canada and around the world, she is delighted to call Newfoundland home yet again. Carrie-Jane—who also responds to "Ms!"—teaches newcomers to Canada in the K-12 system in St. John's. "Past Tenses" is her first work of fiction and first creative publication.